Other Books by Carol Shackleford

THE WINDOW TRILOGY

The Underwater Window

The Discovered Windows

The Broken Window

ADA GRACE

Happy reading!
Carol Shackleford

LOOK FOR ME

IN THE

SHADOWS

By Carol Shackleford

Chapter 1

Staring out the small window of the 747, Leah wondered how long the airline could actually hold you on a plane against your will. Certainly, the delay was understandable with the storms outside, but this was getting ridiculous. Leaning her forehead against the cool plastic of the window's edge, she stared out at the lights reflecting off the water puddles and the bright halos surrounding the headlights of numerous miniature vehicles maneuvering around out in the pouring rain. There was no chance that anyone's luggage would be dry on the carousel at the baggage claim. Luckily, Leah had everything she needed on her carry-on. Her eyes made their way up a few rows to the header above row 18. She just wanted to grab that bag and head out the door. Unfortunately, not only was the plane still out on the tarmac waiting for an available door, but she was also not yet at her final destination. She was supposed to arrive at the house by eight o'clock this evening and that included the 30-minute drive after retrieving her car. Glancing at her smartwatch, she realized there was no way that would happen. With a deep sigh, she moved her head back to the window's edge and watched the drops of rain run slowly down the window. How did the drops go so slow when the rain was coming down so hard? That must be physics or something and she was never very good at that type of stuff.

Leah didn't know how long she had been concentrating on the slow-moving rain drops but she jumped enough to be embarrassed when the pilot's loud, staticky voice came over the intercom announcing there was a door coming available in the next couple minutes. He reminded everyone to check their connecting flight because many had been delayed or cancelled. Everyone started grumbling and complaining as they pulled out their phones and confirmed his bad news. Leah moved her hand along the zipper of the purse she had been holding in her lap the entire flight. There was no use taking out her phone to check the information. She had her paper ticket tucked inside, and she had memorized the flight number. Every time she tried to look at information on the internet, she felt more confused than when she started. It was better to just wait and check the big screen in the overcrowded hallways of the airport.

Starting to feel antsy, her foot began bouncing up and down. It was one of the many nervous quirks she did not even realize she was doing. With her toes planted on the floor, her heel bounced up and down to no particular rhythm. She noticed the older woman sitting next to her cast a disgusted look in her direction, and Leah quickly put a stop to it with a quiet, "Sorry." The woman hadn't spoken to her the entire flight which was perfectly fine with her. Leah felt bad for the woman who seemed to get annoyed at each person who walked by or at anyone talking a few notches above a polite tone behind them. Leah thought the woman would come unglued when a baby started crying a half dozen seats in front of them.

Crossing her ankles in front of her, Leah had to attempt to focus on something else. She hated sitting with her feet on the ground. She had a terrible habit of always sitting on her foot. First one, and then the other. She would curl her leg at the knee and either sit on her foot or prop it against her opposite thigh. It was certainly considered undignified, but a habit is a habit and it was hard to break. Antsy is what she named it. Fidgety. She wasn't uncomfortable. Just never comfortable. She knew that if one wasn't a fidgety person, there was no explaining it. You were either antsy or you wouldn't understand. Switching feet to cross her ankles the other way, she tried to relax her mind. She knew she had no control over her current situation and that in and of itself made her antsy. Soon she would be off this plane and one step closer to a comfortable bed. Promising herself that she would never fly alone again, she was among the crowd as they were united in positive, verbal language when the plane slowly started inching its way forward. While she thought cheering was a bit over the top, she couldn't help but smile at the quick change of attitude. 'We do love getting what we want, don't we?', she thought. She thought even the cranky lady next to her possibly had a lighter tone when she exclaimed, "Finally!" for everyone to hear.

One step closer. She watched out the tiny window again as raincoat-covered crew waved bright flashlights in the air to seemingly direct the plane. Could the pilot actually see them from so high up in the air? Well, however it got done, she was glad someone was willing to stand out in the cold, drenching rain to help them arrive safely at their gate. As usual, her over-analysis of situations made her watch and wonder about several of the people making their living out in the weather. Were they happy? Did they like their job? Were they married? Did they have a nice cozy home to go to at the end of a long, hard day? Were they comfortable with their decisions? Stop! She had to quit. Closing her eyes, she imagined a list of numbers. Not very many things in life were certain but numbers always were. They relaxed her. They calmed her mind. They equaled. They balanced. You can't say that about very many things.

As the plane arrived at the exact spot it needed to be, the door hadn't even been opened yet when everyone stood up and started reaching overhead or pushing into the aisle. Seriously. Wouldn't it be much easier if each row just waited until the row in front of them was up and out? This was simply chaos. Why couldn't everyone just realize that chaos will end up taking longer and getting you more worked up? She made herself just breathe. Think about the simple math. Forty-eight minus one and a half was forty-six and a half. Forty-six and a half wasn't bad.

Chapter 2

Eventually the plane cleared out enough for Leah to depart her seat and make the slow journey in line up the aisle and out the door. Feeling the cold, damp air blowing through the break in the gap of space between the jetway and where it touches the plane's exterior felt refreshing after being on that stuffy aircraft for so long. Inhaling slowly, she grabbed as much fresh air as the crowd would allow before continuing to the terminal. She noticed a young woman carrying a small child and trying to pull a suitcase with a travel sized duffle bag on top of it. As she got closer, Leah couldn't help but see that the woman was pregnant. Glancing around at all of the passers-by, she felt saddened by the lack of acknowledgment of this woman's situation. She was obviously struggling. Slowing her pace,

Leah walked alongside the young woman and asked timidly, "Can I help you? I could carry your bag or something." Leah felt a tiny stab of nervousness because she already knew her connecting flight would be difficult to make on time, but she didn't feel right not offering her help.

The young woman looked toward her. Her glance was past her and downcast, not into her eyes. Leah was surprised she even noticed the lack of eye contact since she was also guilty of not being good with direct eye communication.   The woman answered quickly and quietly, "No, thank you. We're fine." She held her child tighter and tried to walk faster.

Not being able to help her wandering thoughts, Leah thought of several different possibilities of why this woman, hardly an adult herself, would be traveling alone with a small child and one on the way. It never ceased to surprise her how many thoughts could go through her mind in such a short amount of time. Reprimanding herself, she told herself to mind her own business and start worrying about her own situation which may very well include missing her flight. Looking up and down the hallways, Leah looked for the nearest signage to point her in the direction of her new gate. Walking toward the big flight board to verify her information, she was surprised to see all the lines that read "Delayed". With a feeling of heaviness, she located her flight only to find that not only was it delayed, but it had been moved to a different gate. Looking around, she had a hard time believing all of these people milling around and walking with purpose in every direction actually knew what they were doing. Did none of them feel as overwhelmed as she did? Reminding herself that she would never fly alone again, she took a deep breath and started in the direction she thought she had to go. It appeared that she had several hours to kill so she was in no big hurry.

Whether it was a good thing or bad, she didn't know. Leah could notice nothing and everything at the same time. If someone asked her to describe the cranky woman who had been sitting next to her on the plane, she would have to be vague. Older. Short, gray hair. Nothing else. She had no idea what the woman had been wearing or if she was wearing jewelry. Nothing specific. But Leah could describe in detail the feeling of love between the elderly couple holding hands and walking slowly down the long, bustling concourse. There was no need to talk between them because neither of them could probably hear over the commotion around them. Leah could tell you about the look of frustration on the man's face as his kids pushed each other and tried to make each of their demands known about where they preferred to get a snack. She could describe the lack of communication between so many people who were obviously traveling together but couldn't get off their phones to have a conversation with each other. She had no details but an overabundance of information bouncing around in her head.

Arriving at her temporary destination, she verified the information on the display board near the boarding door from which she had just exited. She was surprised to learn her departure gate was just a few gates away from where she stood. That was extremely lucky. Looking around, she chose a seat as far away from everyone as she could get. Not one for striking up a conversation with a stranger, but equally not fond of the information her phone could provide, she sat down alone with her thoughts. Leah would catch herself staring out into space and wondering what people thought when they looked at her. No one probably even noticed her sitting quietly, not making eye contact with anyone and just blending into the background. Did her posture show her tenseness? She would be sore tomorrow from the strain of her rigid poise. Crossing her legs, her foot bounced slightly to an erratic beat. There was noise everywhere but nothing she could make out particularly. There were TVs with shows that didn't seem to match the voices that were playing overhead. However, most of it was constantly being talked over by the updates from the gate agents talking into a microphone behind the desks. This was usually followed by loud grumbles and several people filing over to the desk to make their complaints heard.

Leah glanced at the time on her wrist and was contemplating whether to get something to eat. The seats around her were filling up with people waiting for the same connecting flight. She overheard many phone conversations involving relief over making it to the plane on time followed shortly by complaints about the delay. One brief look out the window explained the problem, but it was hard to believe that rain could turn everything to a standstill. The airlines probably knew something the passengers didn't. She would just have to be patient and trust the system. Never one to be patient for long, Leah rummaged through her purse and pulled out a book and a small notepad with a pen. Along with numbers, lists were a good source of relaxation. Staring out the wall of windows, she got caught up in the activity outside. She recognized one of the baggage handlers out in the pouring rain. He had worn a large raincoat but she remembered him because under his hood, he wore a neon yellow colored stocking cap that came down almost to the middle of his eye brows. Even though it was dark and becoming foggy, she could make out his eyes. They reflected the lights from around him and when he looked up from his task, she noticed the expression that shown from his eyes. His eyes looked very kind and it seemed like they were squinted at the corners as if he was smiling. It was so nice to see someone enjoying their work even under such unappealing conditions. Looking further out, she saw the man that had directed their plane in with the flashlights. Leah smiled as she watched him dancing in the rain. She wondered what type of music he was listening to. Whatever it was, he was sure having a good time. Looking around at her fellow travelers, she couldn't say the same thing about them. Everyone looked miserable.

Turning her attention back to her book and note pad, she picked up her pen. Holding it at one end, she began tapping the loose end against her remaining three fingernails. Realizing she was just fidgeting again; she tried to focus on her list. It just wasn't going to happen.

17

There were way too many distractions. For a split second, her mind wandered to a memory of her husband, Dallas, teasing her about squirrels. Every time her mind wandered and she flitted off in a direction other than where she was headed, he would say, "squirrels". It wasn't uncommon for Leah to start talking about a subject then get off on four different topics before finishing with the question, "What was I saying?" She believed he thought it was endearing but to her it was just plain frustrating. She really couldn't help it. Picturing him in her mind made her long for him to be here with her. Everything would be so much easier. He was so easy-going and could stay calm in every situation. The complete opposite of her which is probably why they got along so well. Determined not to start getting melancholy, she pulled herself together. Knowing it would be a waste of time trying to read her book, she put it back in her purse along with her blank list and pen. Standing up and lightly kicking the bottom of her carry-on suitcase to the pull behind mode, she started a slow walk down the hallway.

Looking at all of the destinations as she walked by each gate, she was aware of how many places she had never been. That was fine with her. She really preferred her own home. Her comfort zone as she liked to refer to it. Getting to the end of the long concourse, she looked to the right then to the left. Then she turned on her heel and headed back in the direction from where she had come. Slowly making her way back to her gate, she watched people rushing in every direction. Some planes were still taking off despite the weather. As she was passing the gate that supposedly would take passengers to Fargo, she noticed an elderly man sitting alone in a wheelchair. He had dropped his hat down by the back wheel. It was just out of his reach. He stretched as far as he could with a look of discomfort on his face. Walking quickly to his side, Leah leaned down, picked it up and handed it to him. Sitting back upright, the man tilted his head back to look up at her face. "Thank you, young lady," he said.

Feeling a smile spread across her face, she replied, "Young lady! Well, aren't you sweet. Did you drop your glasses too?"

He grinned. "Compared to me, everyone is young."

"Well, I will take it as a very nice compliment. Thank you." Leah sat in the chair closest to him so he didn't have to look up at her. "Is there anything I can get for you?"

Tilting his head to study her for a second, he answered, "My mouth is a bit dry but I don't dare drink too much before the plane ride. You wouldn't happen to have a mint or something, would you?"

Unzipping her purse, she happily replied, "There is a reason I carry this huge purse. It has almost anything you could possibly ask for." Leah pulled out a snack-sized baggie. "Not only do I have a mint, I have a selection. I have a peppermint or I have cough drops or a butterscotch. Name it and it's yours."

With delight, he exclaimed, "Well, I haven't had a butterscotch in years. That would be perfect."

"It's yours." She handed him the butterscotch. "And now, here, you take a peppermint and a cough drop for later if you need it." She waited for him to unwrap his candy before trading him for the empty wrapper. He slipped the extras into the front pocket of his worn flannel shirt. Closing his eyes for a brief time, he savored the taste of the butterscotch.

"I used to arm wrestle my brother for these." He chuckled at the memory. Reaching out his arm, he extended his hand. "My name's Benjamin. Some call me Ben. I don't care much for Benji."

Returning his firm handshake, Leah said, "Benjamin, it's nice to meet you. I'm Leah."

"Leah, you headed to Fargo?"

Pointing down the long, crowded hallway, she answered, "No. My gate is down that direction. My plane doesn't leave for a while so I was just wandering around to kill some time."

"Well, I'm glad you did. I think I was about to pull a muscle in my back trying to reach my hat. Thank you kindly for your help."

"Of course." Leah leaned back in the chair, feeling more relaxed.

Tipping his head toward the window, Benjamin observed out loud, "Still pouring down out there. I hope we don't get delayed too long. According to that billboard, it says Fargo is clear and cold. Pretty normal. Hope I make it before it gets too late. Hate putting people out. No one likes picking up at the airport."

"I'm sure whoever is picking you up is happy to do it." Leah assured him.

He grunted a non-response before asking, "What about you? You have someone special picking you up?"

With a slight sigh, she replied, "No. I have my car parked in the lot. I'm only about 30 minutes from the airport so it won't be bad." Deciding to change the subject, Leah started asking him questions about his travels and they had a lively discussion which helped pass the time.

She noticed that when she was distracted, she didn't worry so much about everything. Maybe it was a good thing that her mind could only focus well on one thing at a time.

Chapter 3

Peering over the top rim of his non-prescription glasses, Dale observed the impatient passengers across the crowded hallway who were waiting to board the plane he would be on shortly. He could watch them better from over here. Pulling the knot of his tie a little looser, he felt annoyed at the delay. Choosing to dress as a businessman with a suit now seemed like a terrible idea. He had to admit that he was pulling it off quite nicely though. Yesterday's smooth shave left his face feeling cool and bare. After having the minimum of at least a scruffy beard for several years, it was hard to get used to the new feel. Turning the un-read page of the newspaper which he had purchased at the airport gift shop, he wondered who in the world actually read this boring stuff. He didn't know why anyone would care about any of this.

Getting back to his observations, he was not feeling optimistic about the chances of finding a perfect candidate to help him follow through with his plan. Maybe it was time to think of a Plan B. Feeling anger build inside, he tried to calm his thoughts before they started taking over. It never ended well when his thoughts started taking over.

Wearing a beat-up old sweatshirt and jeans with an actual wear-hole in the leg, Agent Ryan sat patiently in the midst of tourists, travelers of business and plenty of children of all ages. Most of the children were on phones regardless of their age, but several were running uncontrolled and seemingly unsupervised around the open areas while receiving plenty of irritated looks from already annoyed people. Several frazzled parents were trying to quiet crying babies or fighting siblings. With a feeling mixed with sympathy for those around him and thankfulness that his days of having to maintain control of his own children when they were this age were behind him, he leaned back and kicked his leg up to place his ankle on the opposite knee. He could see Dale in the distance checking out the passengers around him. Off in the distance, he heard over the sound of all the commotion, a woman's gentle laughter. Making a quick sweeping glance off to his right, he noticed her several doors down sitting next to an elderly man in a wheelchair. Never letting his glance rest on her, he continued to scan the crowd. Pulling his mind back to the task at hand, he wouldn't let anything or anyone distract him during this important mission.

Leah could tell that Benjamin was getting tired. He could hardly hold open his drooping eyelids. Patting his hand, she winked at him as she stated, "I'm going to see if I can shake things up around here." She left his side to ask the attendant at the counter if they had any updated information about the flight to Fargo. Right as she was about to step up to the desk, the attendant picked up the speaker and gave Leah a cold look as she announced to the waiting passengers that the plane would begin boarding in 20 minutes. Everyone started moving things around and gathering their belongings as if she had just said 20 seconds instead of minutes. Thinking to herself that it would be a long 20 minutes, Leah made her way back to Benjamin who was grinning at her.

"You sure get things done," he stated with pride.

Chuckling, she sat down. "What can I say? I have power." Looking down the still crowded concourse, she wrinkled her nose and blinked her eyes. It reminded Benjamin of the old 'I Dream of Jeannie' show on tv. "Let's see if I have the same power for my flight." With a laugh and a shrug, she raised her hands in the air as if giving up. "It's out of my control, which of course, I don't like. But I'm sure I'll get home eventually. It has been an absolute pleasure to meet you, Benjamin."

With gentle, age-worn eyes, Benjamin looked at her for a second before replying, "Thank you for noticing me, Leah. Thank you for talking with me. Most folks don't take the time any more. I do appreciate it." He reached out to shake her hand.

"Well, they are missing out." She shook his hand then placed her hand on his arm and patted it. "Will you be ok getting on the plane?"

"Oh, yes. Don't you worry about me. You better make your way to your gate so you don't miss your own flight."

Laughing, Leah said, "Wouldn't that be something! I think I may run down and get a cup of coffee to keep me going for a while." Standing up, she grabbed her rolling suitcase and purse and headed toward the coffee stand.

While she was waiting in line to order, she looked down at her luggage. It was just your ordinary, standard-issue, rolling suitcase in the exact size to qualify as a carry-on. It allowed just enough room for a few days' worth of travel. There was nothing special about it. She looked at the luggage tag attached with a clear zip tie. Flipping it over so she could read the address, she looked at the numbers and words written on it. She was not feeling homesick for this address. Quite the opposite. It almost made her feel sick to see it. She was lost in her thoughts and had to be tapped on the shoulder from the customer behind her in line. "It's your turn," the lady said rather politely as she pointed to the clerk at the cash register.

Feeling herself turn slightly pink from a blush of embarrassment, she nodded a quick thanks with a smile as she stepped up to order her coffee. The address side of the luggage tag was still facing her as she slowly made her way back toward her destination. As she walked past the Fargo departing gate, Leah noticed with happiness that someone was pushing Benjamin in his wheelchair towards the jetway door. It lifted her mood as she continued her slow pace while blowing on her coffee before taking a careful sip.

The seating area had almost filled up to capacity. Deciding to sit close enough to see and hear any updates on her flight, she took a seat across the way and set her coffee on the floor near her suitcase. Even though she knew she was in the right place, it still made her feel better to double check. She reached into her purse and took out her paper ticket. She looked at it then up at the flight board. She read it quietly to herself. Placing the ticket safely back in her purse, she leaned down to get her coffee and blew on it again before taking another sip. Without leaning all the way back in the chair, she held her purse in her lap and let her mind wander, all while listening closely to everything going on around her. She didn't notice there were eyes watching her every move.

Dale had been fuming about making a Plan B. As the annoying voice announced yet another flight delay over the intercom, he noticed a woman nervously digging into her purse. He watched as she pulled out a paper ticket. Who printed their ticket these days? He saw her look at her ticket and check it against the board. He could read her lips as she read the information. Could he be so lucky that she was on his flight? Taking a quick study of her surroundings, he realized she was alone, at least for the moment, and she had a carry on that would have to go in the overhead bins.

He tried not to stare as he continued to monitor her movements. She was fidgety and anxious. Constantly looking at the time and re-positioning herself in her seat, she looked absolutely uncomfortable in her surroundings. Just what he was looking for. Starting to blink rapidly, he tried to formulate his plan. Squeezing his eyes shut tight to calm himself, he slowly opened them with his gaze directed at her. Squinting in disbelief, he realized she had a baggage tag on her carry-on. He almost felt sorry for her. She was a target for anyone with bad intentions. Well, they would have to get in line. She was exactly who he needed.

He couldn't allow her to move seats before getting her information. He picked up his newspaper and with purpose walked right past the trash can next to him and over to the one just past her. As he came near her bag, he was about to read the address on the tag when one of the out-of-control kids who had been playing tag with several others swerved to miss him and ran into the bag, knocking it into the woman's leg which in turn made her jump and spill her coffee all over her pants and purse. With a look of disbelief, she quickly stood up to assess the coffee spill. Not wanting to draw any attention to himself, Dale quickly turned in the other direction and made his way to another trash can as if it was his intended destination. Meanwhile, the boy's mother started yelling at him from against the back wall row of seats. It drew everyone's attention which Dale was relieved about. Walking into the restroom to remove himself from the area for a few minutes while the dust settled, Dale was repeating over and over in his head the address he was able to retrieve from the luggage tag before the commotion began. Tearing off a piece of paper towel, he pulled a pen from his suit jacket pocket and wrote it down before he forgot. Looking at his reflection in the mirror for several seconds, he returned the pen to its place and put the address in his front pants pocket. Smoothing the lapels of his jacket, he stood a bit taller with the renewed confidence he had in his mission. This was going to work just fine.

Agent Ryan stayed in his seat watching the commotion going on around him. Obviously, it was only a matter of time before one of those kids ran into someone. It's a shame they had spilled coffee. Well, it would come out in the wash he guessed. He had been watching Dale and was slightly impressed with his new look. It was the first time he took on the look of a businessman. Personally, he didn't think it looked entirely convincing, but then again, he knew Dale's history and what he was capable of.

Keeping track of his surroundings, Agent Ryan appeared relaxed as he kicked back, crossing his ankles in front of him with his arms crossed over his chest. The person sitting right behind him was watching a tv show on their phone with the volume on high. It was hard to believe that people were so self-centered. At least it was a show he was familiar with so he could picture what was going on while listening. Maybe it would help pass the time until his flight. As he made himself comfortable, he noticed Dale coming back to the seating area. He also couldn't help letting his gaze wander in the direction of the woman who had spilled the coffee. Not allowing himself to get distracted with her, he let himself get wrapped up in the comedy unfolding behind him on the tiny, loud six-inch screen.

Leah was getting restless. Planes had begun to take off with the storms passing through, but the area was still crowded and people were starting to get tired and more annoyed with each passing hour. Digging through her purse again, she pulled out a granola bar. There was no use getting hungry since it tended to make her a bit irritable. Standing up and pushing her fists into her arched back, it felt good to feel it pop. Throwing her purse strap over her shoulder, she pulled her suitcase behind her as she began pacing. Even though she could see that it would still be over an hour before boarding began, she didn't have it in her to leave the general area. She walked three gates down, turned around and went past the seat she had been sitting in to walk three gates in the other direction. After doing this several times, she walked to an open area to look out the window. It was now dark in a different way. It was night-time dark instead of stormy dark. Although it had quit raining, it was starting to get foggy. The workers were busy in every capacity outside. Watching the difference in each person's demeanor, she could tell who was doing a good job and who was just killing time until shift change. Trying to imagine herself doing each of the tasks she was observing, she decided that she much preferred to work indoors. She wasn't a fan of heat, humidity, getting wet or bugs. There had to be plenty of bugs out there. Thank goodness there were people willing to work outdoors.

Leah could see inside the windows of the plane that had been boarded for quite a long time but still waited at the gate. The lights from the interior of the plane allowed a unique look into the lives of its group of impatient passengers. As she slowly passed her gaze over the various heads and faces that were in each window, she stopped when she saw the young woman who had been walking with the small child when she first got off her plane. She was staring out the window and had big tears rolling down her face. Leah could tell they were quiet tears because her face held no emotion. However, the expression in her eyes was heartbreaking. The sympathy Leah felt for this stranger was overwhelming. She should have tried harder to help her. With a shift of her eyes, the woman looked through the window right into Leah's compassionate study of her. Leah lifted the corners of her mouth into a small smile of encouragement. The woman kept her eyes locked with Leah's for what seemed like several minutes. Without a blink or change in expression, she reached up and slowly pulled down the plane's window covering.

Feeling the heavy weight of a new mental burden, Leah sighed and started playing with the strap of her purse. She peered at her hands wringing the worn leather strap. She took note of the plain look of her hand. It looked wrong without her wedding ring. With a feeling of panic rising inside, she started thinking of her simple numbers.

Forty-six and a half minus two and a half equals forty-four. Forty-four now seemed like an impossibly high number. This wasn't helping. Trying a different tactic, she started making a list in her mind of what she had to do when she arrived home. Looking down at her lap, the first thing on her list for the morning would be to wash the coffee out of these pants.

Chapter 4

The desk attendant had everyone's attention when she lifted the phone by her computer and listened to what was said regarding the flight. Her expression didn't give anything away as she reached for the transmitter and spoke unrushed into it. It seemed as if everyone, including the energetic children held their breath waiting for the verdict. The flight would begin boarding in 20 minutes. Please have your phones or tickets ready to be scanned. People in first class or anyone with small children would be first to board. They had overbooked the flight so anyone who would be willing to give up their seat, please go to the desk to arrange for a later flight along with a voucher for a hotel along with another ticket of your choosing in the future. Most people having flown before already knew the drill. There was a palpable feeling of relief over the group and almost instantly the mood changed to one which was much more agreeable.

Dale was glad to be moving forward with his plan. He didn't need any more distractions. He was getting so close to completion. Nothing was going to stop him now. His confidence sank to the pit of his stomach when he saw his chosen subject heading toward the desk. She couldn't offer to give up her ticket. That would mess everything up. He was about to get up in order to distract her when she swerved to the left and headed for the restroom. Waiting a few moments to see if he could relax back the building tension that he could feel rising in every part of his body, he felt some relief when she came back and sat in one of the seats of the edge of the crowd. Some people were already starting to get in line. He wondered why anyone would want to be on that plane any longer than necessary. He had to plan his timing just right in order to have un-noticed access to her bag. He would try to board the plane with about five people in between them.

Trying not to let his concentration wander and lose track of the plan, he couldn't stop himself from having a quick reel of memory run through his mind of his time spent behind bars. They were never able to get any information out of him and his contacts were able to see to his release in a relatively short amount of time. But there was no denying what it cost him to be trapped with no escape. Staring at the woman who would help him complete his plan, he knew he would do anything, anything at all, to not step foot in a prison again.

Dale didn't even notice that he was not staring but rather glaring at the woman. Fortunately for him, the loud speaker distracted his attention away from his dangerous thoughts. He stood up to proceed to the end of the boarding line. He typed his password into his phone in order to pull up his boarding pass to scan. Irritation rose up the back of his neck and he found it hard not to scream at the person in front of him who was so busy talking on the phone that he knew they would not be ready to show their boarding pass. He imagined what it would feel like to punch this person in the back of the head and he began to relax a little with thoughts of inflicting pain on someone. Feeling slightly better, he almost felt a small smile reach his lips. Almost.

Agent Ryan was still kicked back in his chair watching passengers anxiously waiting in line. Certainly, most of them were tired and past ready to be home. He could tell which ones were positive and optimistic and which were the opposite. There was nothing like flight delays to show people's true character. He was ready for this day to be over too, but he was just in the beginning of this new and hopefully final phase of his assignment. He knew it was going to be a while before he would truly be able to completely relax.

Sweeping his gaze over Dale but not resting on him, Agent Ryan was almost stunned at the fierce look in his eyes. No one on this flight was safe with the hostility he knew Dale possessed. With a renewed reminder of his purpose for this operation, he stood up and slightly stretched his tight muscles to prepare for the cramped awaiting flight. Like a trained penguin, he slowly went to the back of the line and stood patiently for his turn. The woman behind him tapped him on the shoulder to ask him if he thought she had time to run to the restroom before the last boarding call. Wondering why in the world people waited until the last minute to think about things, he tried to be polite in his response of having no idea. Fingers crossed that he wouldn't have to sit by her on the plane. He was patient and friendly but there was a limit for everyone, wasn't there?

Leah was gripping her ticket so tight that her hand was sweating. It seemed like there was chaos everywhere. She took one last look outside and noticed the rain had started up again. Hoping it wouldn't delay her flight any longer, she took several steps forward in the slow progression towards the boarding door. She had an image in her mind of cattle being herded from a pasture into the back of a waiting truck. At least the livestock didn't understand

43

what was waiting for them at the other end of the line. She only had an empty house. That understanding was upsetting. Standing still for a minute, she couldn't help but sway back and forth. She often noticed men standing completely still. What was it about women that made them sway? Before she had too much time to think about it, they were on the move again.

Eventually they wound their way around the curve in the airway and she could feel little sprays of water making their fight through the small slits of connection. Entering the plane, the air was already feeling stale and heavy. Following closely behind the person in front of her, she looked at the seat number on her ticket at least a dozen times. It wasn't because she couldn't remember but rather out of a habit of doubting herself and double checking.

Finally, she arrived at her seat and set her purse down before pushing the handle of her carry-on into itself and hoisting it up over her head. She had chosen a completely empty compartment across the aisle from her seat. Of course, it would fill up before everyone was seated but she liked knowing that she had a good spot. That would make it easier when they arrived at their destination. It was always a bummer to have to go backward to get your bag. With some satisfaction of making it this far, she sat next to the window in the cramped, small commuter plane. She leaned her head back against the headrest and tried to resist thinking about who else recently had their head on the same headrest. Not worried about bothering anyone at this point of the flight, she let her nervous leg bounce as she held her purse in her lap and closed her eyes.

Dale was several passengers behind the woman. He watched her place her carry-on bag across the aisle from where she took her seat. With pleasure, he noticed plenty of room in the compartment next to her bag. Someone had placed their bag right next to hers. He slid it over and slipped his carefully in between the two. That was easier than he had expected. He took his seat four rows behind the woman and kept a close eye on who else was coming down the aisle to make sure no one messed with their bags. He acknowledged his brilliance in making certain to get a seat toward the back of the plane so his target could remain constantly in his line of vision.

Just as he was getting comfortable, a man who stood about six-foot-five came and stood next to him. "Excuse me, but I have the seat next to you. You wouldn't mind moving over so I could sit on the aisle, would you?" With a chuckle he continued, "These legs are hard to squish into tiny spaces."

Moving his legs to the side to indicate the inside seat with a nod of his head, Dale responded, "Well, you should have paid up for first class then."

With a slight nod of agreement, the man climbed over Dale as gracefully as possible and squeezed into the tight spot by the window.

Dale didn't give the other man's discomfort one second of thought as he huffed at the inconvenience.

Agent Ryan quietly took his seat in the back row of the plane and took note of his surroundings. The plane was full and everyone was anxious to get to their destination even though it was much later than expected. He went through in his mind all of the information they had on Dale. It was amazing to witness him so-called "blending in" with those around him. He wasn't that sharp of a guy so why had he eluded them for so long? Today was the day though. They had everything they needed to finally get him. Now it was just a waiting game. Waiting with delays made it so much longer.

The flight had been uneventful which was much appreciated. They had dimmed the lights and Leah could hear several people quietly snoring and one individual not so quietly snoring. Thankfully he wasn't too close to her. Her eyes were mostly shut but she kept a slight watch on everything through a small, practiced opening. She even had her head tilted slightly to the side to make it look like she was sleeping. She never wanted to feel like she wasn't in control of her situation. Certainly, falling asleep on an airplane was a prime example of not being in control. Not making a move of awareness, she didn't even stir when Dale got up from his seat behind her and made his way to the overhead compartment. Through the small slits of her eyes, she could see him open the compartment, take something from his bag, move a few things around, and without making any commotion, he took out a pair of earbuds and quietly shut the compartment door. He made his way back to his seat and she completely closed her eyes and instead used her ears to observe everything around her. There was not much activity going on since everyone was so exhausted.

Before she had time to get too fidgety, the pilot came over the loud speaker to tell everyone to prepare for descent. The nappers woke refreshed and there was the slight buzz of excitement to begin the next stage of their journey. Looking out her window, Leah barely noticed the moon's light reflecting off the small lakes and ponds that could be seen as the plane's wing tipped toward the direction of the airport. The weather appeared to be clear and the air looked crisp. As they continued to get closer and the chatter in the cabin started to rise, she could see the full moon shining its light off a lake she had never even realized was so close to town. As she stared into the water, she wondered what went on under the dark glassy layer of mirrored light. She was sure there were stories to be told about the activities under the transparent, crystal water. She smiled to herself as the pilot reminded everyone to buckle their seatbelts. Why would anyone take it off during the flight? Turbulence could happen at any time. The flight was so short, they hadn't even offered beverages. That was fine with her. She was ready to get off this plane. As the wheels touched down and everyone was forced forward in their seats, she looked up the aisle leading to the front of the plane. She took a deep breath and held it for a few extra seconds before slowly releasing it. Turbulence really could happen at any time.

Agent Ryan was glad this part of the trip was over. Luckily the passenger sitting next to him slept the whole time and didn't want to exchange needless chatter during the flight. He had watched with interest as Dale got up and took the product from his bag and moved it to the one next to his. Dale was getting so confident; it was almost ridiculous. He was even so careless that he took his earbuds out of his bag and once back to his seat, he just put them into his pocket. Even a rookie agent would have been able to recognize that sloppy maneuver. This guy was about to get what was coming to him. Soon they would have possession of all the information they had been searching for.

Chapter 5

Being a small plane, departing the aircraft didn't take as long as it had earlier. Walking through the door into the terminal, Leah looked around the empty building. It appeared deserted. Through the glass, she could see the area outside lit up just slightly with a few late workers already pulling luggage off the plane and throwing it onto the cart patiently waiting to carry it to the worn-out passengers. Certainly, the workers were as ready to get home as everyone else. Glad that she didn't have to wait for additional luggage, Leah slowly pulled her carry on behind her and headed to the exit door behind which her car sat waiting for her in the always full parking lot. Twisting her wrist towards herself, she waited for her old smartwatch to light up with the current time. Letting out a frustrated sigh, she looked around for a clock. Not immediately seeing one, she stepped to the side of the slow flowing traffic so she wouldn't be in anyone's way. She twisted her wrist again. Nothing. Why did this darn watch light up with just a slight wrist movement in the middle of the night, blinding her in the darkness of sleep, but when she wanted it to work, it often let her down? It probably needed to be charged. Reminding herself gently that it was actually probably her fault and she was just being irritable because she was tired, she reached over with her right hand and tapped the face of the smartwatch with two quick taps. Raising her eyebrows in surprise, she allowed herself to feel weary since the time revealed that it was almost 1:00.

Knowing she still had a good thirty-minute drive ahead of her, she stopped off at the rest room to splash just a touch of cold water on her eyes to try freshening up. Leaning forward until her face was just inches from the mirror, her eyebrows raised in surprise along with a slight frown from her worn out, chapped lips. She spoke to herself out loud, "Good grief! It looks like you walked through a desert for a week." Pulling back from the close inspection, she sighed and shrugged her shoulders. "You've got to work with what you've got." Starting to dig in her purse for ChapStick and maybe even some lipstick, she decided it wasn't necessary. "Tomorrow." She yawned and stretched her arms out to her sides as far as she could while arching her back. Staring back at her reflection again, she spoke with more confidence. "Let's make it happen."

As she made her way toward the door leading to long-term parking, she noticed some commotion near the luggage carousal. A lot of passengers had already left the building so it was easy to see through the small crowd gathered around the conveyor belt. Several police officers from three different directions were all heading toward one man just on the edge of the gathering on-lookers. All of the officers had their hands on their weapons and were yelling at the man to put his hands up. As they surrounded him, one officer shuffled the passengers off in the other direction saying that their baggage would be delivered to them outside the exit door. Leah picked up her pace to make it outside quickly in order to not be in the way. She glanced over at the man who was now laying on the floor with his hands being cuffed behind his back. Feeling an icy chill go through her from the split second of eye contact made with Dale, she was certain she had just seen a sneak peek into the evil mind of a mad man.

Dale had been walking toward the baggage claim area when he sensed the air changing around him. He knew they were here. He could feel it. Reaching into his pocket, he wadded up the small piece of paper towel with the address written on it and discretely let it fall to the floor without adjusting his stride. Feeling a charge of energy go through him like an electric current, he was almost feeling giddy that they had finally found him. And they had nothing. He almost laughed out loud.

Laying on the ground with his head on the floor, he looked over at the woman who now carried his information. He looked deep into her eyes and at her face to finish memorizing the last bits. He couldn't help but smile gleefully. They had wasted their time and resources. He got them again. They were so stupid. It almost wasn't a fair fight. Feeling his arrogance taking a victory lap, he watched with smugness as the gloved officer took item after item from his carry-on bag. They knew he hadn't checked any bags so they were certain what they were looking for was in the case the officer was dismantling. Another officer was thoroughly patting him down and checking his pockets, shoes, socks, collar and sleeves. After ripping the seams out of the bag and finding nothing in it or on him, they helped him up off the floor and started leading him to a waiting patrol car.

They had already read him his rights but he didn't need to hear them. He intended to use his right to remain silent. They would get nothing out of him. He knew the drill. They would take him down to headquarters and question him. He would be out before the sun came up. They couldn't prove a thing and they had nothing to charge him with. Another victory to add to the growing collection. Pride made him stand tall before being ushered into the waiting back seat of the cruiser.

Agent Ryan was watching from a distance. It went down about like he had expected. These officers were well trained. With all of the chaos, no one had noticed him quickly bending down to pick the small wadded up paper from the floor. He still held it in his hand as they took Dale out of the building.

Walking out to his car, he stoically got behind the wheel and started up the engine before putting his hands in his lap and opening the paper to read its contents. On the paper was written an address. With a sigh and a slow nod, he put the car into reverse and backed out of the parking spot. He would head to the hotel for a few hours of rest knowing his subject was in the custody of capable people. Although sleep would most likely elude him, he was ready to have some peaceful time to formulate several backup plans for finally achieving a successful end to this long investigation.

Leah stopped outside the opening garage door waiting for its slow access availability. Driving in, she put the car in park and sat there for several minutes. With a feeling of dread, she heavily got out of the driver's seat and popped open the trunk to retrieve her bag. Not knowing if her body or her mind felt heavier, she dragged herself through the door into the quiet stillness of the empty house. Pulling her cosmetic bag out of the top of the carry-on, she left the rest of it in the laundry room. She made her way through the kitchen and across the dark living room. There was a sliver of dim light from the street lamp a few houses down the road coming through the edges of the closed blinds. It was just enough light to guide her way across the house to the bedroom.

Old habits die hard so even though she was exhausted, she still took the time to wash her face and brush her teeth. Pulling down the covers, she slid into the comfortable bed and tried to decompress as the overpowering silence was only interrupted by the ticking of the clock and the random sighs of Leah herself. After ten minutes of restlessness, she rolled toward her nightstand and pulled the picture frame from the small table top. She looked at the picture of herself in front of a waterfall. She was smiling happily. Of course, that was because she had been happy. Taking the back of the frame off, she slid out a picture that had been placed behind the waterfall picture. Feeling tears immediately well up in her eyes, she couldn't stop them from falling as she stared at the picture of her husband with his strong arms wrapped around her in a big bear hug. They were laughing and comfortable in each other's embrace. It was her safe place. Her ultimate comfort zone. And today that was gone.

Tilting her head to one side as she lifted it slightly off of the pillow, she listened carefully. She thought she heard something. She put her head back and tried to relax. Closing her eyes, she remembered her husband saying, "Listen for me in the shadows." As she started drifting off, she whispered into the darkness, "Good night, Cowboy."

She fell asleep trying to imagine the sound of his heavy, deep sleep breathing when he was lying next to her.

As expected, Dale found himself released from police custody by 4:00. He took a taxi back to the airport to get his vehicle. Stopping by a 24-hour pharmacy, he grabbed what he needed and walked to the checkout. Not giving him a second glance, the cashier rang up the small ream of printer paper, packing tape, a small mailing box, a pair of jersey gloves and a 12-ounce bottle of orange juice.

Arriving at a halfway presentable motel, he checked into his room and took the supplies in along with the duffle bag he had in his trunk. He had assumed the police would hold his luggage, so he had prepared ahead of time. It's not like he hadn't learned some tricks along the way. He sat at the small desk table and opened his bottle of orange juice. Putting on the gloves, he opened the ream of paper and took out a sheet. He took the pen from his suit jacket before standing up and pulling off the jacket. Wanting to throw it across the room, he decided instead to go hang it up on one of the two hangers on the short rod above the mini-fridge. Taking his seat again, he wrote in all capital letters the message he was going to deliver. Satisfied with the wording, he opened up the flat cardboard into its box shape and used the packing tape to secure it into formation. He placed the note inside the box and taped the top shut. Leaning back in the chair, he finished up the orange juice and threw it across the room towards the trash can. Bouncing off the wall, it landed in the empty can. Dale thought to himself, "He scores. Again."

Agent Ryan got in a very quick power nap before rising and going out to run. He hated running. But for some reason, people ignored runners. If you were walking, people thought you were looking for something. Being truthful with himself, he had to admit that running might have been a stretch. Maybe a slow jog would be a better description. He wasn't as young as he used to be and some days, he really felt it. The purpose of his run was to verify

Dale's movements. He had received the information with the motel room number and his vehicle license plate. As he was arriving at the driveway entrance to the motel, a dog came out from behind the fence running along the property line. He was a big dog with a very loud bark. Especially at this time of morning. The bark pierced the still air. Agent Ryan had several choices but quickly analyzing them in his mind, he made a swift decision. Stopping in his tracks and hoping with everything he had that this was a friendly dog, he waited with trepidation as the dog charged him. Almost as startled as Agent Ryan when the dog started barking, the dog seemed equally startled that his target had quit running. Skidding to a stop in front of him, the dog sniffed the air. He must have realized that he was in good company because he started vigorously wagging his tail. Ryan seized the opportunity to make his observations. Reaching over with an open palm for the dog to sniff, he saw Dale's car in the parking lot. It was easy to see since there were only a few cars around. Presuming that since Dale was in room 6 and the car was parked by the sixth door from the left, he assumed without having to see the number on the door that it was the correct room. No lights were on and there didn't appear to be any activity in or around the room. It figured that he would be able to sleep with everything going on. It was probably easy to sleep when you didn't have a conscience keeping you awake. With disgust at the thought, Ryan gave the dog one last good scratch behind the ears and continued on his slow jog. He held the belief that nothing good went on after midnight. However, by six in the morning, things were starting to wake up and he didn't want to draw any attention to himself.

Hearing a dog barking in the near distance was just enough to wake Dale from his slumber. Rolling over, he contemplated going back to sleep for a few more winks. After laying there squeezing his eyes shut to convince them back to doze mode for several minutes, he finally popped them open and stared at the wall. Stupid dogs. He hated waking up irritated. He watched the shadows of early dawn dance care-free off his walls. Figuring that he may as well get the show on the road, he sat up and threw his legs over the side of the bed. Trying to inspire himself he thought about the day. The sooner it started, the sooner he could be on his way to the good life. This payout would be enough to get him started fresh any place he desired. He still hadn't decided on his final destination. He wasn't a pie in the sky kind of guy who dreamed about sitting on a beach in Cabo San Lucas or one of those other fancy places. He would be comfortable in a small cabin in the woods somewhere remote. Somewhere that no one would ever be able to find him. Wondering if he would get lonely being completely alone, he started wondering if he should take someone with him. He didn't care much for animals. They needed too much attention. He didn't have friends and the criticism from his family over his life choices had not been well received. And then it happened. A plan starting forming in his mind. The woman from the airport. She was just supposed to be his information carrier. But what if she was more than that? His heart started beating faster. Loving the anticipation that a new plan allowed, he started thinking about it. The more he thought about it, the more he liked it. Instead of feeling heavy and irritated, he felt light and giddy. Practically jumping out of bed, he felt like there was now a spring in his step. This was going to be fun!

Feeling restless after a very disturbed, short night's sleep, Leah decided to just get out of bed and make some coffee. Maybe that would help get the morning started. Shuffling into the kitchen, she glanced out the window above the sink. There was a peaceful view to be enjoyed and she knew she wasn't taking advantage of the calming start to the day it could provide. Instead of using the window for relaxed viewing, she chose to lean over and unlock the latch. Cranking the handle, she opened the window several inches. It was just enough to let in some fresh, cool air, but not so much as to make it too chilly in the room. Breathing in the refreshing air, she took several deep breaths before taking the few steps over to the coffee pot.

As she began to prepare a caffeine wake up, sounds of several different kinds of birds began filling the room with activity.

Leah took the coffee-brewing time to lean back against the sink and with arms crossed over her chest, she closed her eyes and allowed herself the luxury of memories with her husband. He could carry on a conversation with the birds. He knew what kind they were and could sing their tunes right back to them. He would go out to fill their feeders in the morning and by afternoon, they would take turns knocking on the windows to try scaring away the squirrels who were eating food not meant for them. Getting distracted by voices outside, Leah took a coffee cup out and began throwing in the things that made her coffee more like a morning dessert. Equal parts cream and sugar. She justified it to herself by saying that since she was only having two cups instead of a whole pot, it equaled out to not that much per cup.

Taking her by surprise, the voices from outside came closer and there was a knock on her door. Looking into the laundry room at the mirror against the back wall, she was horrified by what she saw. Although she had thrown on old, worn-out blue jeans and a bulky sweatshirt, she hadn't showered or even brushed her hair yet. She contemplated not answering the door. There was another knock followed by the shrill ring of the doorbell. With a deep sigh and embarrassment tinging her cheeks, she went to the peek hole to look out. It was a man who appeared to be possibly in his mid-fifties with a woman who was maybe in her 80's glaring at him.

Slowly opening the door, she spoke through the screen door. "Can I help you?" Leah asked cautiously.

"I sure hope so," the man answered.

"No, thank you," the woman replied sternly.

Clearing his throat, the man spoke quickly. "My name is Daniel Charter. My mother, Elinore, lives right next door." He tipped his head to the house close enough to throw a rock at and break a window.

"Daniel, this is ridiculous. You can't ask a stranger to do this. I don't need a babysitter." Elinore spoke harshly.

Clearing his throat again, he began his plea. "I'm so sorry to bother you. I know you don't know me but I have a bit of a crisis on my hands and I have a huge favor to ask." He looked expectantly at Leah with pleading eyes.

Not sure how to respond, she didn't say anything.

Taking a deep breath, Daniel began his request. "Ok. Well. Let's see. I know you don't know me. I already said that."

Leah was starting to feel bad for him. "I don't actually know your mom, either."

With a look of surprise, he glanced at his mom and then back to Leah. "Oh. She has lived here for a long time."

"Maybe so, but I just moved in a few weeks ago."

Putting his fingers on his temple, Daniel was trying to think. Nodding and rubbing his head he replied, "Ok."

Leah noticed a white vehicle pull up to the stop sign across the street. She was aware that the driver was wearing a hooded jacket pulled over his head so she couldn't see what he looked like.

Distracting her away from the vehicle outside, Daniel began his story again, "Ok. Well, like I said, I'm in a bit of a crisis. Well, maybe not a crisis but definitely an emergency. At least a predicament. You see, usually my mom has a caregiver since she has a bit of trouble with her 'memory'." He said the word 'memory' in a whisper.

Elinore rolled her eyes. "I'm standing right here, Daniel, and there is nothing wrong with my hearing or my memory. This is embarrassing and unnecessary. Just go and I'll be fine." Addressing Leah, Elinore said, "I'm sorry to bother you, dear. My son is over protective and is overreacting to nothing. We'll leave you now."

Daniel stood firm. "Mom. Please. This is important."

Elinore's eyes got bigger and filled with expression. Leaning around Leah, she looked past her and into the living room. "Is John here?"

Agent Ryan arrived at the office eagerly anticipating the latest word on the investigation. It was now just more or less a waiting game. He grabbed an exceptionally disgusting cup of coffee from the break room. Who could even make a pot of coffee this bad? Sitting around the conference table listening to the re-cap from last night's arrest and interrogation of Dale, the thick, murky coffee left a taste in his mouth that almost made him sick to his stomach. This guy was unstable. Anything was possible. Agent Ryan knew Dale felt like he had nothing to lose. He knew Dale was feeling more and more confident with each passing day. The investigators were on their game. The undercover officers were all top-notch. He just couldn't shake the feeling that things always had a chance of going sideways. He thought about the paper with the address on it that Dale had discarded. Swallowing hard, he could

feel the furry sludge left at the back of his tongue. This
was going to be a really long day.

Chapter 6

Elinore was looking past Leah into the living room. "John? Are you here?" she hollered into the empty space. She leaned around Leah to get a look into the house.

Leah looked with confusion from Elinore to Daniel. She tried to come up with a question to ask but came up blank. Apparently, the look was received because Daniel looked at her then to the ground.

Putting his hand on his mom's back, Daniel said, "Mom, he's not here. That's not why we're here."

Elinore shook his hand off her back. "Well, where is he? He's waiting for me, you know." Looking at Leah, she asked, "Who are you?"

With a questioning look to Daniel, Leah said, "I'm Leah, I think you live next door to me. I just moved in so I haven't met many people yet."

Extending her hand, Elinore reached for Leah's hand. "It's nice to meet you, Leah. This is a lovely area. You are going to love it here." Looking over at Daniel and casting her gaze to his hands, she asked him quietly, "Didn't you bring a house-warming gift to the new neighbor?"

Leah suspected that his patience must be wearing thin as he replied slowly and a little louder than he had been before, "No, mom. That's not why we're here."

Leah could feel Daniel's rising frustration. Feeling a bit sorry for him, she opened her door all the way and motioned for them to enter. "Please, come in. I just made a pot of coffee. I usually only make enough for two cups but I can quickly brew more."

Daniel and Elinore entered and were led to the small table beside the kitchen. Elinore took a seat and Daniel followed Leah several steps toward the coffee pot. "I'm so sorry to bother you." Daniel began with the continued look of near panic on his face. He started talking quickly while it seemed his mom was distracted taking in her surroundings. "I would normally never ask someone for something like this but I'm desperate. My mom has dementia and today is not a good day. Her caregiver didn't show up and they don't have anyone else to send in her place. I received a call from the hospital that my sister was in a bad car accident and is about to go into surgery. It's a three-hour drive to get there. She doesn't have anyone else and I don't want her to wake up alone. My mother's afternoon person will be here around 3:00. Could she please stay here with you until the caregiver arrives?" Finally taking a breath, he looked into Leah's sympathetic face and felt a sliver of hope. "Please?"

Feeling overwhelmed with all of the information Daniel just gave her; she rubbed her hands together. Starting to wring her hands as one of her stress-relievers, she bit her tongue because her first response to any request was always yes. This was not at all something she was comfortable with. The timing was terrible. No. It wouldn't work. "Can't she go with you?" It was all she could think of as a reply.

73

"There's no way. First of all, she doesn't do well in a car even for short distances. Secondly, Amanda is her baby girl. She doesn't even know about the accident. She wouldn't understand. Please, it's just the three of us now. We don't have anyone else. I have to be there for her." With the look of concern still in Leah's expression, he gave one last plea. "I recently lost my dad. My mom is slipping from me daily. I can't lose my sister, too. I know being there with her might not make sense to you, but it's just something I have to do."

Feeling pressure, Leah didn't know how to say no. Hesitantly, she asked, "It's only until 3:00?"

Nodding vigorously, he replied, "Yes. And it's just today. I promise." Before Leah could change her mind, Daniel spoke to his mom, "You are going to stay here and visit Leah for a while. I have to go but Janice will be here this afternoon."

Looking at her surroundings, confusion clouded her expression. "What? Where are you going?" She looked at Leah then back to Daniel. "I don't know her. I'll just go home. No need to bother a stranger."

Leah quickly thought to ask for his phone number along with the home healthcare number in case she had any questions. He quietly slipped out the front door. Feeling the weight of responsibility heavy on her shoulders, she decided the least she could do was make Elinore as comfortable as possible. "Elinore, would you like something to eat for breakfast?"

Elinore hollered through the house, "Danny, hurry up. You're going to be late for school." Looking back at Leah she asked, "Do you have any children, dear?"

"I do. Three. But they are grown and not at home anymore."

Nodding at the motherhood bond she just made with Leah, Elinore said, "Danny likes a quick piece of toast with peanut butter. If you have that, I would have a piece also since you're already getting it."

Feeling positive that at least she was doing something productive, Leah happily agreed. She turned

75

on the radio that sat on top of the microwave in the corner of the cabinets hoping to distract her company so she had time to think. As an old Ray Price song floated through the air and the aroma of bread toasting to a light crisp filled the kitchen, a look of remembrance crossed Elinore's face.

"John and I used to dance to this song every time we heard it. No matter where we were. The kids used to tease us something fierce."

Leah smiled at her new friend's fond memory which was triggered from the song floating through the air. Setting the plate of toast with peanut butter in front of her guest, Leah took the seat across the table from her. "I love Ray Price. His music just makes you feel good."

Eating her toast, it seemed as though Elinore was content at the moment. She swayed back and forth in her seat sometimes humming along with the music. When the song finished, she looked at Leah then down at her plate of crumbs. Leaning across the table she whispered, "They won't give me toast when they come to the house. They steal my food. I have to hide some it from them. Don't tell them I told you."

Feeling heartbroken for this woman she didn't even know, Leah held her finger up to her lips. "Your secret is safe with me."

Elinore nodded and started humming to the new song playing in the background.

Getting up from the table, Leah grabbed the plate of toast crumbs and carried it to the dishwasher. Today was already going to be complicated enough. What had she gotten herself into?

Dale couldn't chance sitting at the stop sign any longer. He looked again at the house numbers on the mailbox. He was definitely at the right house. Who were these people standing outside the door? He could see through the glass storm door that it was actually the woman from the airport. With disgust, he drove off. He was going to have to postpone his plan a little longer. He despised waiting. Deciding to go grab some breakfast before trying again, he felt a little more relaxed as he began thinking through the tough choice between pancakes or French toast.

He was not three blocks from her house when a siren bleeped behind him. Looking in his rear-view mirror, Dale swore as he looked down at his speedometer. The officer flashed his red and blues and bleeped his siren again. Pulling off to the curb, he waited impatiently for the officer to approach the car. Hitting the button to lower the window, he clenched his right hand into a fist then relaxed it several times in an effort to reduce his anger. As the young man stepped up to the side of the car, Dale was relieved to see that he didn't recognize him from last night. That would have been really bad luck. Knowing that no matter his mood, it always paid to be polite instead of aggressive, Dale addressed him in a friendly voice, "Good morning, Officer." He gave a forced, fake smile.

Giving a nod of acknowledgment, the officer asked, "Any idea why I pulled you over this morning?"

With a chuckle a little too loud, he replied, "Not a clue."

"You were going 35."

Feeling the heat of anger rising up, he tried to keep his cool. "Really? Surely you can help me out and give me a break for five over?"

Nodding in understanding, the officer replied, "I would really like to, but it's actually a school zone so the speed limit is 20."

Looking at his surroundings, he started to argue. It was his nature after all. "I don't see any kids walking around."

"That's not really the point, sir."

"Well, what is the point then? That's a stupid law when there aren't even kids around and you got people like me trying to get someplace and have to slow to a crawl for what? Nothing!" His voice was rising with every word.

The officer held up his hand and nodded. "Trying to get someplace this morning?" he asked with friendliness?

Lies coming quickly to his mind he chose his favorite. "I am heading to the hospital to see my grandma.

She has taken a turn for the worse and I might already be too late." With a big sigh, his words dripped with sorrow, "I really wanted to say good bye."

With compassion and understanding etched across his face, the young man looked into Dale's eyes and said, "Well, you best be on your way then. I'll give you a break this time, but slow down, especially through the next several blocks of the school zone. I sure hope you make it in time." Raising his hand in the air, he dismissed Dale to continue on his way.

"Thank you, Officer. I sure appreciate it. Have a good day. Be safe out there." He put the car into drive and slowly pulled away from the curb. Stupid fool. Reaching into his pocket, he pulled out a bottle of pills and with the skill of much practice, was able to remove the lid with one hand. He slid two tablets into his palm and threw them into his mouth. Rolling up the window, he looked at himself in the rear-view mirror. He smiled and said to himself, "You still got it."

Waiting for Dale to drive down the road, the officer radioed into headquarters. "I got him. Very hot and cold. Quick temper. Nothing in the car except a cardboard box in the seat next to him. I think he's ready to lose it."

Leah asked Elinore if she wanted to watch something on tv while she tended to some things. Saying she wouldn't mind catching up on some news, Leah got her settled in the living room before heading to the hamper to take out her coffee-stained pants. Was it possible that this spill just happened last night? It seemed like days ago already. Even with the tv on in the background and a stranger on the couch in the other room, Leah felt the emptiness of being alone. The uncertainty of the next couple of days was closing in on her. Uncertainty was her enemy. She liked certainty. Routine. A schedule you could rely on. Pulling her mind back to her task at hand, she walked the pants and several other items from the hamper to the laundry room and started the washer. Trying to look on the bright side, she thought about the good things with having Elinore here. It would help her pass the time until this afternoon. Nothing would happen before mid-day anyway, right?

Dale's cell phone rang. He answered it with a curt, "Yes?"

The voice on the other end was calm and deep. "Report."

"It's taken care of. I'll have it to you tomorrow."

The line went dead. Jerk. Dale was annoyed by the lack of appreciation. Pulling into the parking lot of a fairly large diner, he started thinking again about the possibility of having a companion with him at his little cabin in the woods. It would be nice to have someone there to cook for him and keep him company. She would be so lucky to be part of his plan. He was almost jealous of her. She would get all the benefits of his hard work. She probably wouldn't understand his plan right off the bat so he would have to explain it to her later. After he ate his hearty breakfast of French toast and pancakes, he would drive by her house again to see how hard it would be to enter unnoticed into her home. He loved making choices. The choice to not choose between two breakfast items by getting them both. The choice of taking her from her home or from the park. It was turning out to be a good day.

Agent Ryan had his hands balled into fists as he paced the room. He couldn't stand the length of time a whole day could be. He had so much riding on this case. Too much. It was way too personal. He thought he would be ok with it but he wasn't. Dale was too unhinged. Too capable of anything. At first, he thought it was a slam dunk but the more he observed Dale at the airport, the more he became uncertain of their decision. Had they made a terrible mistake? He couldn't allow anything to happen.

Almost as if his thoughts had been spoken out loud, his chief walked into the room and closed the door behind him. "There's not time to change your mind now. We're way too far in."

Feeling the reality of the words sinking into his thoughts, he let out a loud burst of air. He didn't realize he had been holding his breath. "Right. I know."

"You need to lay low and not let your emotions get in the middle of everything. We have worked on this for too long for your personal feelings to mess everything up," the Chief spoke with force.

"I agree with you. We have all our bases covered. Nothing can happen. We got him. I know we do. The waiting is just hard."

The Chief left the room. Agent Ryan looked up at the clock. Was time going backwards? This was going to be the longest day of his life.

Chapter 7

Not coming as a complete surprise, the news was nothing but depressing and negative. Elinore seemed to have no idea about any of the topics that were being covered. That was probably for the best anyway. Trying to come up with something to do to help pass the time, Leah asked Elinore if she would like to get out for some fresh air and enjoy a short walk around the block. Elinore agreed and they headed out into the sunshine.

They had only made it a few houses down the block when the neighbor who was outside sweeping her porch called out to them. "Elinore, is that you?"

Leah looked up at the cheerful, plump woman as she leaned her broom against the side of the house and came vigorously down her sidewalk towards them.

Elinore looked at her with a warm smile although she didn't say anything. The friendly woman looked with curiosity at Leah. "Are you a new caregiver? I don't recognize you from before."

Before she could get too far ahead of herself, Leah stopped the questioning. She reached out a hand as a welcoming gesture and stated, "Hi. My name is Leah. I am your new neighbor." Pointing to the end of the street, she directed the woman to the house she was living in.

Her curiosity piqued; she gladly grabbed the offered hand to shake. "Oh, Leah! It's so nice to meet you. I wondered what the story was with that house. You see, it had been on the market for a while and we just thought maybe there was something wrong with it. Is there anything wrong with it?"

Leah gently changed the subject. "I'm sorry. I didn't get your name."

"Oh, of course. I'm Laverne. You know like on Laverne and Shirley? Although I really kind of liked Shirley better. Did you ever see the one when Laverne accidentally steals a scarf and they put her in jail? Can you imagine? Jail? But of course, they make it funny but it wouldn't really be funny." She took a breath to keep on with her story but was interrupted by Elinore.

"We must get on our way. Nice to see you." Elinore linked her arm through Leah's and practically dragged her a number of houses further down the street.

Leah took advantage of the opportunity to make their escape. It would be nice to visit some of the neighbors, but she had too much on her mind to be very outgoing at the moment. She didn't want to give a bad impression of herself.

Elinore stated, "You know, she'll be waiting for us to walk past again. We better just go around the block and come in from the other side."

With a chuckle and a grin, Leah replied, "I do believe you have an excellent idea."

They walked in silence looking at, as well as listening to, the birds and an occasional dog barking or car driving past in the distance. They pointed out different lawn ornaments and Elinore stopped for several minutes to look at a small statue of a girl holding a basket of flowers. "There's something familiar about that statue. I just can't put my finger on it."

Leah agreed with her. "She's cute. Looks like a hard worker."

Elinore made a sound of approval before continuing on their way.

During their whole walk, no one drove past. "It's pretty quiet around here. Are most of the neighbors retired?" asked Leah.

"No. A lot of us have kids the same age. It's nice for Danny to have kids to play with. His sister doesn't like to be outside much. She would rather be reading inside. Do you have any children?"

"I do. It's too bad they never got to play together. I bet they would have been friends." Leah said. She looked around the neighborhood. This would have made a nice place to raise a family. Not allowing herself to get melancholy, she noticed that Elinore was slowing down.

They were almost back to the house but it hadn't crossed Leah's mind that it might be too much of a walk for her if she wasn't used to it. Sticking out her elbow towards Elinore, she offered her arm expecting it to be rejected. Surprise mixed with pleasure as Elinore took her arm and they walked the remaining distance together. It seemed as though Elinore must feel some sense of comfort or trust with Leah which made her happy.

As they turned to walk up the sidewalk, a chill ran through Leah as she noticed the same white car at the stop sign. Still wearing the hooded sweatshirt, she couldn't see his face. However, she did pay attention to the license plate and tried to store it in her memory to write down when she got inside. As they approached the house, both ladies noticed the cardboard box on the front step. It was just inches from the door so there was no way to open the door without first picking up the box. Knowing she hadn't ordered anything, she turned the box over in her hands. There was no weight to it. There were also no markings on the box. It appeared to be a brand-new box. Like the kind you would buy at a store to mail something. Her name and address weren't on it nor was there a return address. Looking up and over to the stop sign, she was glad to see the car was now moving on.

Elinore seemed happy to see the package. "I love getting mail. Did you order something fun? Maybe a new blouse?"

Tucking it under her arm, she opened the door and let Elinore in first. As soon as the door was shut behind them, she locked it. Unsure what was in the mystery box, she didn't want to open it in front of Elinore so she said, "Make yourself comfortable. I have to go move the clothes from the washer to the dryer." As Elinore went into the living room, Leah grabbed the pair of scissors from the utensil drawer and went around the corner to the laundry room. Cutting the tape on the box carefully, she set the scissors down on the dryer and opened the flaps one at a time. Inside was just a single sheet of paper with handwriting on it. Reading it quietly out loud she let the paper fall back into the dark recess at the bottom of the box. Starting to feel jittery, she stared out the laundry room door into the kitchen. Making out the time on the front of the oven, she shook her head. This was bad. Her gaze landed on the small suitcase in the corner of the room. Left there last night in her exhaustion, it loomed large in the room now. Wanting to shut it all out, she had to make due with closing the laundry room door behind her and trying to remember to breathe so she could figure out how in the world she was going to handle this. The wet clothes remained forgotten in the washer. The license plate number now a distant memory not to be recalled.

Why was there an old woman with her? She better not get in the way. He had no time for changes of plans or wrenches being thrown into the mix. Not sure what to do to kill time before the meeting, he decided it was best not to drive around town. Who knows what the outcome would be if he were pulled over again? Better not to take any chances. He chose to go to the library to search for remote homes. He didn't necessarily want to be off the grid but maybe for a while that would be the best situation. Specifically searching homes that were for sale by owner instead of listed through a real estate company, he figured he could work a cash deal very quickly. He had narrowed his search to a location about 400 miles from where he now sat. Assuming that he wouldn't be able to go home in order to gather his belongings, he would have to start his new life from scratch. Never caring much for the name Dale, he could become anyone he wanted now. His boss would provide him with a new identity after receiving his end of the bargain.

Finding a piece of scratch paper on top of one of the bookshelves, he jotted down the information from three of his top home choices. After deleting his search history, he left the library with fresh energy. Using what he referred to as his "work phone", he called the numbers from his property picks. One was sold, one went right to voice mail and one said they were eager to sell and would look at any reasonable offer. Feeling another boost of confidence, he made an appointment to view the property in two days.

Stopping at a discount store, he filled his cart with essentials like some cookware, a few dishes, some clothing, hygiene supplies and bedding. He didn't know what his new home would come furnished with, but he would have to lay low for a while so he tried to think of everything he might need. As he headed toward the checkout, he suddenly realized that he had totally forgotten about supplies for his guest. Not sure what would be needed, he picked up a hair brush, tooth brush and two dresses that appeared to made from sweatshirt material. They certainly looked like they would be comfortable for her. That should be all she required for a while. Stopping off at the hardware section, he grabbed some duct tape, zip ties and a rope. He loved these stores that literally had everything you needed in one place. As the cashier rang up his purchases, he noticed her looking at him when she rang up the dresses. He smiled and said cheerfully, "They're for my wife. I hope I got her the right size."

That seemed to break the ice, because the cashier smiled back and replied, "She'll love them. I have one and it's really comfortable."

Walking out to the car with bags overflowing the cart, he thought about the word wife. He had only thought of the woman as company to pass the time and someone to cook for him. But the more he thought about it, the more he liked the idea of her being his wife. She would be so pleased.

Agent Ryan asked for the investigator to repeat what the cashier had told him. "Wife? I didn't know he was married. It's nowhere in his file. Do you suppose they are estranged and he is planning to go to her after turning over the information?"

The investigator replied, "I suppose he has to go somewhere. That's as good a place as any if he wants to stay under the radar for a while."

94

"Check into it. Dive deep if you have to. This makes no sense. Although nothing he does makes sense. Let me know the second you find anything." Also, find out what he was doing at the library. Being left alone in the room with his thoughts, Agent Ryan paced the small space trying to understand how they could have possibly missed this. It didn't add up. Something wasn't right. He went to the conference room which had been set up to monitor the situation. Reaching his hand out, he took the headphones. Slipping them over his ears, he listened closely to the slightly muffled silence.

Nothing was going quite the way it had been planned. And he didn't like it. He didn't like it one bit.

Elinore was dozing on the couch when Leah entered the room again. She had called the number for the caregiver and they were no help at all. She understood being understaffed but this was an emergency. Daniel's phone had gone straight to voice mail. There was no need to leave him a message since he couldn't be any help from so far away at this point anyway. Sitting down in a comfortable chair facing the window, she felt anything but comfortable. Looking out the large frame of sparkling glass, she took in the view from outside. From here she could see the house across the street and the one directly next to it. She had not seen anyone at either. Their houses had closed curtains and no lights shined out in the darkness when she had gotten home from the airport. Of course, it had been late so that was to be expected. Her corner house was the last one before the road ended in a T at the stop sign with heavy woods across the street in that direction. She had only seen the one car several times but other than that, there was no traffic on this street. Everyone must prefer to leave the neighborhood from the other direction. It suddenly made her feel very isolated and exposed.

Although the sun shined brightly and there was not a cloud in the sky, Leah felt the darkness of fear and uncertainty. She would do what the note said but with only two hours, what would she do with Elinore? When was she going to learn how to say no? She got herself into this mess and obviously she couldn't leave Elinore here alone. She couldn't make any other phone calls in case the note writer was somehow listening. Never in her life had she known the true understanding of the word paranoia, but at the moment she was almost afraid to breathe in case she was being monitored by the lunatic who had written the note. Getting out of her chair, she went to the window and closed the shades. It felt creepy to think he was possibly watching her.

Walking by the living room where Elinore continued her peaceful nap on the couch, she stopped to watch the woman for a minute. Even though she had only known her for a few hours, Leah already felt a strong feeling of protectiveness over her. She looked to be about the age her mother would have been. Trying to imagine what Elinore had been like when she was younger, Leah felt certain that she had been very strong and determined. Probably a bit intimidating, really. But now here she was on Leah's couch being vulnerable and innocently yet

97

defensively unaware of her surroundings. That must be an awful prison. Possibly more so for her loved ones who remembered who she used to be.

There were so many lessons to be learned here, but unfortunately, Leah didn't feel like she had the luxury to explore them. She tried to take a moment to carefully put her thoughts about the matter in the back of her mind to ponder over more thoroughly when she was not so distracted with the task at hand. If she was going to get in a shower today, it would have to be right now. She kept one ear keenly attentive for any movement in the house while she took the quickest shower since her children were small.

Dale was pacing in his motel room. He looked around with disgust. This place was nasty. He was trying to lay low until the meeting time. Would she show up? He was sure she would. He had observed her timid nature. She was someone used to doing what she was told. Hopefully she wouldn't put up too much of a fight when he told her she would be coming with him. The surprise of his request would throw her off. If she protested, he would be ready with the chloroform. He had used it before and it worked like a charm. It would feel different this time because he would be able to keep his prize instead of turning her over to his boss like he had always done in the past. He felt the same adrenaline rush that always came with the job but this time was even more exciting knowing he would be complete when it was over. More money than he knew how to spend, a home of his own, and now the picture in his mind of him and his wife living happily ever after. He had never dreamed he would come so far. Who could ever make this up? Feeling himself swelling up a bit with pride, he felt he was finally getting what he deserved after working so hard all these years. Yes. He was finally getting what he deserved.

Leah watched as Elinore opened her eyes slowly with the drowsiness felt upon first waking. Feeling a bit nervous about her reaction of being in an unfamiliar place, Leah didn't say anything and waited for Elinore to notice her sitting across the room.

Elinore rolled her head around a bit to work out the kinks that had developed from sleeping while holding her head up. Still feeling a bit dazed, she noticed the friendly face starting at her. Elinore smiled ever so slightly and asked in a quiet, raspy, still sleepy voice, "Do you remember when the world was written in cursive?" Closing her eyes again, her smile grew. "That was a great time to be alive."

Leah got up from her chair and walked over to take the cushion next to Elinore. She reached over and picked up a frail hand. Speaking gently to her new friend who still had her eyes closed, she replied, "I do remember. And some days you can still find a bit of that world out there. You just have to look harder than you used to." The frail hand squeezed hers and Leah smiled at the delicate strength of her grip.

Popping open her eyes, Elinore looked at Leah and said with the enthusiasm of a child, "Do you have any cookies?"

"Surely, we can find something in the kitchen. Let's go see what's in there." She stood up and held out her hand to help Elinore up off of the low seat of the couch. "What do you want to drink with our snack? Coffee, milk, water? I'm not sure what else I have in the fridge."

"Do you have any tea? I love tea and," she lowered her voice to a whisper, "they won't make it for me. They tell me it's too much work."

Leah felt her heart wilt at this statement. "Well, that's just silly. It's only boiling some water." She pulled out two boxes. "Would you like Earl Grey or Orange & Spice?"

"Just whatever you're making for yourself, dear."

Deciding to just set the tea bags on the table to let Elinore decide if she really did have a preference once the water was ready, she opened the pantry door to see what there was available to snack on. "It looks like all I have to choose from are graham crackers or Milano's. I also have some pretzels but they are already open so they may be getting stale."

"I haven't had a Milano in years. That sounds wonderful." She looked at Leah then down to the table where the cookies and tea bags sat. Looking back, she stared at Leah for minute before asking, "Who are you?"

With a pleasant smile, she answered, "My name is Leah. I'm your new neighbor. Maybe over our tea, you could tell me about the neighborhood."

"Certainly, dear." The stories went on for quite some time. It was nice to have the distraction but Leah kept glancing at the clock on the microwave. It would be time to leave soon. Sometimes she felt like she did better under pressure so it was probably good that she hadn't had the time to over-think her situation. She would just grab the suitcase and go to the meeting place.

As the time loomed near, Leah said, "I'm going to go freshen up and then I thought we would go for a quick drive to see what's going on in town."

"No. You go ahead. I don't really like car rides," Elinore sounded resolute.

Not only was this unexpected, but it was unnerving. She was unprepared for this complication. Why hadn't she thought this through? Why had she said yes to letting Elinore stay here for the day? Feeling frustrated, she tried a different strategy. "I could really use your help. I have to get some groceries and being new to town, I don't remember how to get to the grocery store. Would you go with me to help me find my way?"

"Well, the town isn't very big so you probably wouldn't get lost." Looking into Leah's desperate eyes, she relented and finally said with some annoyance. "I suppose that would be all right."

Able to breathe again, Leah quickly shuffled Elinore into the car before she could change her mind. She ran quickly back into the house to grab the suitcase and tossed it into the back seat before backing out of the garage. As she drove past the elementary school, she noticed the kids playing outside. It must be recess for some. She felt heaviness weigh on her even as she watched the carefree games of tag and pushes on the swings. Whoever would leave such a note of demand was not a stable person. And now, not only did she have to worry about herself, but also about the elderly woman sitting next to her telling her where she thought you had to turn to get to the grocery store.

Everyone was in their place and each person knew their role. With so much on the line, Agent Ryan had been ordered to stay in the surveillance room and just listen and watch the events play out. He was still trying to rein in his anger at not being given clearance to be on scene. His whole body ached with tension as he watched on high alert as Dale parked his car and made his way to the walking trail. The camera angles weren't perfect and he lost sight of him several times. Each time feeling his heart skip a beat until he came into the next camera's frame. Leaning over and squinting at the screen, he spoke through his communication device. "He has something in his hand. A piece of a shirt or towel. Not big but definitely something. He's up to something. Be alert. He's a slimy one."

Chapter 8

Dale had parked his car in an area with a couple other vehicles. The trail wound through thick trees and even if there were other people out here, the odds of them being on this one section at the same time were slim. He had told the woman to park at the next parking area over. It was close enough to throw a stone if the woods had not been there. He was getting close to the meeting spot when he heard a woman yelling. He couldn't quite make out what she was hollering but it could no doubt draw attention to the area. Cursing under his breath, he picked up his pace and had just made visual contact with his new wife when the woman who was yelling came out from the next parking area and right onto the trail behind her. Stopping in his tracks, he realized he recognized the woman. She was the one walking with his wife this morning. Why would somebody be so dumb as to bring along a witness?

Leah froze. She had seen Dale. Last time she saw him his face had been pressed into the floor. She saw him the same time she heard Elinore. Elinore had been agitated when they didn't go to the grocery store. Leah was mad at herself for not thinking this through all the way. She had pleaded with Elinore to stay in the car for just a minute while she dropped something off not 100 yards away. Even if Elinore had gotten out of the car, Leah had figured she wouldn't be able to get far enough away that she couldn't be spotted in a few minutes. Her biggest concern had been if Elinore would trip on the uneven trail and fall. How would she live with herself if her friend broke a hip or something? Like she didn't have enough to worry about. She hadn't expected this. That seemed to be the theme of the day. Being unprepared.

Elinore was making her way along the uneven path and through the grouping of trees leading to the trail.

She had panic in her voice. "Daniel? Amanda? Where are you?" On the verge of crying, the fear rose. "Daniel! Amanda! Why did you wander off?" She was nearly hysterical after just 20 seconds. Leah set the suitcase on the ground and gestured to it as Dale got close. She turned to leave and noticed him doing the same. She ran to Elinore and tried to soothe her. She helped the woman to the only bench in sight and tried to calm her down. After several minutes of reassurance and gently rubbing her back, Leah asked Elinore to walk with her for one minute and then they would go home. Not in a frame of mind to argue, she went along like the lost soul she was. Rounding the slight curve in the trail, she stopped and felt the color drain from her face. The darn suitcase was still sitting there.

Agent Ryan used language that was not typically in his vocabulary as he frantically tried to make sense of what just happened. "Is the subject still in sight?" he asked to anyone with an answer.

The reply came back with hesitation. "He left the area without the case. I repeat without the case."

Agent Ryan had seen it happen. Dale obviously got spooked by the woman's rant. This was unquestionably a setback. "And the case? Is it still in possession of the carrier?"

"Yes, sir."

Rubbing his hand across the scruff of an unshaven chin, he had to wonder just how far back this had set them. He had all but promised a deadline. He couldn't go back on that. But really, what choice did he have? The ball was definitely not in their court. They had to wait on the unsettled thoughts of a mad man. The reality of that made his pulse throb from the backs of his eyes to the top of his head.

Dale couldn't believe what had just happened. His palms were sweating and his hands trembled. This was unacceptable. Slamming his fist against the top of the steering wheel, he could hardly focus on the road through the rage distorting his vision. He wasn't about to lose everything he had worked for over this disastrous unforeseen circumstance. Trying to calm his nerves, he kept reminding himself that he sometimes didn't make the best decisions when he was this angry.

Knowing he had to now come up with a completely different plan while still allowing the outcome to arrive by tomorrow in order to keep his boss happy, he knew two things for sure. One, he had to turn the music up on the radio. And two, he had to go through a drive thru and order a double cheeseburger with fries.

Leah was stunned and unsure how to proceed with her day. Elinore was completely over her outburst and it was as if it had not even occurred. At least she just had a few more hours before the home health aide arrived. She could feel the presence of the piece of luggage in the back seat. What was she supposed to do now? Would he come to the house to get it? The thought made her throat want to close. She could leave it on the front step by the door right where he had left the box. That way he could take it and not even have to communicate with her. No. What if someone else happened to see it before him and take it? She didn't think that would happen in the peaceful little town but crazier things were happening every day.

As she passed one of the local drive-thru restaurants, she spotted his car and almost slammed on the breaks. Speaking out loud, she said, "He's right there at the drive-thru window."

"What, dear? Are you hungry for that kind of food? It's not very good for you but it tastes mighty good sometimes."

"I'm sorry. I didn't realize I spoke out loud. It's a bad habit. Just wanting to hear myself talk, I guess." Leah tried to lighten the mood. "Are you hungry?"

"No. Is Wheel of Fortune on yet? We have to go get John so he can watch it. He never misses it. He is the best guesser. I always tell him he should try out for that show. But he tells me then he would be a movie star and he couldn't be responsible for all the other ladies trying to catch his eye. You know, once I caught his eye, it was over. It was love at first sight for the both of us. Do you know what I mean, dear?"

With a sigh, Leah agreed with her. "Yes. I do know."

"So, let's go get John. Is he at the house?"

"No. We'll just go back to my house for a while. Do you like to play cards? I think there must be a deck of cards somewhere around there. What do you say?"

"I do like playing cards. If I can remember how. I might need a refresher course. What are we playing?" Elinore seemed interested.

"I'm not sure. Let's see what we can find and go from there." Leah always swore she wouldn't wish time away but she really wanted to wish this day over. For a million dollars she couldn't begin to predict how this day would end.

Stopping in the office at the motel upon arrival with his lunch, Dale asked the attendant if he could have an envelope. The young man looked in a few drawers and cupboards before he finally found one. What kind of idiot doesn't even know where supplies are kept? Everyone around him was so incompetent. What if he had been so worthless? One thing was sure, he wouldn't be about to be living his dream. Feeling energized with the thought, he went to his room and turned on the tv to entertain him while eating his burger and fries. Once finished, he took out a sheet of paper and found his pen to write yet another note. This was taking longer than he initially thought but sometimes victory was sweeter if you had to work extra hard for it.

He called the front desk. The idiot said he got off work at 4:00 and for $20.00 he would absolutely deliver the envelope to anywhere in town. With that settled, now all he had to do was wait. At this time tomorrow, they would be well on their way to their new home.

Not locating a deck of cards, Leah and Elinore played several hands of Skip-bo instead. Some games didn't take long to remember how to play. They chatted as old friends but in the back of her mind, Leah was on edge. From her seat at the table, she could see out the front window and fully expected to see the white car with tinted windows driving down the street. It made her shiver.

"Are you cold, dear? You should get a sweater. You look a little pale. Are you feeling all right?" Elinore sounded worried.

"Yes. I'm just fine." Leah almost jumped right off her chair when her phone rang. "Hello?" she answered in an unsteady voice.

"This is Janice from Home Health Care. Daniel said to call you when I got here. I'm sorry I'm a little late."

Flipping her wrist and feeling a boost of confidence that her Smartwatch showed the time on the first try, she was surprised at how fast the time had passed playing cards. That had been a good distraction. "Ok. We'll walk over as soon as we finish up here."

With suspicion, Elinore asked, "Who was that?"

"That was Janice. She's there now so you can go back to the comfort of your own home. Thank you for visiting with me today. It's been a pleasure getting to know you."

With a look of sorrow spreading into her eyes, Elinore asked quietly, "Do I have to go?"

"Don't you like Janice?" Leah asked. Her mind was screaming at her to just leave it alone and mind her own business. She had enough to worry about without adding this woman's problems to her list. But her heart wouldn't let it go.

"No. It's not that. I think she's probably ok. Everyone just treats me like a child. Like I can't make any decisions for myself. They act like I'm so fragile that I'll break if they do something wrong. But you treat me like I still have a brain. I've missed feeling like an adult."

Nodding with understanding, Leah commented, "That would be frustrating. Does it help to remind yourself that it's just because they love you and want to protect you? I know I just met you, but I just know you

116

have done so much for others over the years that it's ok to let them do what they can for you now. It might be the only thing they know to do." Leah winked at her. "Even if it does get a little overbearing sometimes."

"I suppose you're right. Would you come to visit me once in a while? I would like knowing someone is making sure they aren't driving me crazy." Elinore made the request with a little hope in her voice.

"I absolutely will. I promise. I'll bring the tea," said Leah, feeling good about making Elinore happy.

With a delighted smile, Elinore got up from the table with Leah and headed back to her own home. Leah couldn't help but wonder if her new friend would remember her the next time they saw each other. With the thought of that possibility, she held on for an extra few seconds when she hugged the woman tightly before leaving her in the care of Janice.

Dale felt relaxed now that he had his new plan in place. He dropped off the envelope at the front desk for the kid to deliver. With the series of threats and the look of fear on his young face, Dale had no doubt the kid would keep this delivery just between the two of them. Well, three if you wanted to count the woman. He had been accused many times in the past with being obsessive but this time he might actually be able to acknowledge it even to himself. He couldn't get the woman off his mind. Getting into his car, he decided to just drive past her house to see if he could get a quick look at her. He hadn't been able to read her expression at the drop off point earlier. He would have actually preferred to have seen absolute fear, but he didn't think that was what he saw. It all happened so fast that he couldn't seem to put his finger on it.

As he came up the street, creeping ever closer to her house, he noticed the isolation of the neighborhood. No one was outside in their yard or walking on the road. No one was driving past. He rolled down the window just a few inches. He didn't hear the sound of any mowers, barking dogs, music or voices. Dale started thinking that his plan should have been to just come here to get his possessions. The suitcase contents and his wife.

Once he started second guessing his choices, he became angry with himself. His good mood was changing quickly. He didn't realize he had been sitting at the stop sign for so long. Sometimes when he let his mind wander, he lost track of time. When he shook himself back to awareness, he looked out his windows and into his mirrors. Great. Someone was coming up the street behind him. He turned left and slowly drove by the side of her house. He hadn't seen her in the window and the house was closed up tight. It would have been nice to see her outside. As he drove slowly, he looked into the rear-view mirror and saw that the car behind him had pulled into the driveway across the street. Well, it was better to go with the initial plan anyway. Last minute changes sometimes had a way of blowing up on you. He would see her soon enough.

Dale drove around town looking for a new meeting place. The irritation from additional planning was giving him a headache. He stopped in the parking lot of a vacant, old building. It appeared to be an old car dealership. Skirting the building, he pulled to an area near the back. Rolling down the window, he took some deep breaths of fresh air as he opened his pill bottle and threw a few into his mouth. Leaning his head back against the dirty headrest, he listened to the sounds around him. Perking up a bit, he realized he hadn't seen any cars drive past. People who didn't know him might think of him as not very knowledgeable. But he had a lot of experience under his belt. He was actually quite good at what he did. After all, he had made it his career. Whoever said a life of crime didn't pay, didn't know anything. It was about to pay. Big time. Tilting his head slightly to the side, he listened intently. Even though it was the middle of the day, he couldn't hear a thing. Nothing at all. Well, call it luck or call it skill, he had just chanced upon a perfect location. He observed his surroundings with more scrutiny. No cameras. No traffic. No people. It would be dark when she came to meet him.

Almost feeling giddy at his good fortune, he began to think about what his life would be like with a little money, a new house in a new state and a new bride. He didn't feel like he was an exceptionally picky person but as his new-found luck would have it, he was pleased to realize that the more he thought about her, the more he realized how beautiful she was. They would make such a perfect pair. When they eventually were able to go places together, people would look at them together and be jealous. Yes. It was all falling into place. With his headache almost gone, his new plan fully formulated, and his new wife just hours from his arms, he was feeling more confident than ever. Nothing could stand in his way.

Chapter 9

Leah paced the house feeling caged and claustrophobic. There was nothing she could do until she was directed on the next step. She was too nervous to leave the house. Even though she didn't have an appetite, she knew it wouldn't do any good to get jittery from low blood sugar. It didn't happen very often, but when it did, it made her feel terrible, so she grabbed a can of soup and some saltine crackers and began her quick meal prep. Usually, she rather enjoyed the quiet, but at the moment, it felt overpowering. While the soup warmed on the stove, she walked into the living room and channel surfed until she landed on what looked like it might be an 'Everybody Loves Raymond' marathon. She had seen every episode so many times that she figured it would be a brainless way to pass time with enough distraction to keep her mind somewhat busy.

With the noise of the tv and the soup and crackers balanced in her hand, she sat on the couch and tried not to look at the wall clock every 30 seconds. This day could not possibly go any slower. She was just about to take her last bite of soup off the spoon when the doorbell rang. She jumped enough to spill the spoon full of liquid onto the front of her shirt. With a sigh of irritation, she didn't understand why she kept spilling on herself. Most likely it was just a case of the jitters. Setting the bowl onto the coffee table, she quietly went to the front door and looked out the peek hole. There was a young man standing on the other side of the door looking impatient. He pushed the bell again.

Without opening the door, Leah called out, "Can I help you?"

Staring at the door with a look of confusion, he leaned forward and spoke as if into a microphone. She figured he must have thought there was one of those devices around allowing the person inside to see who was at their door. In a loud slow voice, he enunciated each word, "I have an envelope that I was told to deliver to you."

Taking a deep breath to calm herself, she opened the door and looked closer at the boy. He didn't appear very comfortable with the situation. That made two of them. She cracked open the storm door and reached her hand out of the small space she had allowed.

He handed her the envelope and was about to turn around to leave when he stopped short. He made eye contact with her before speaking quickly. It appeared as if he was saying what he wanted to say before he changed his mind. "I don't know what the deal is but I'd watch your back. He has a problem." He turned and ran down the sidewalk and across the street to his tiny, beat-up car. It was slow to start, but once it did, he couldn't get out of the neighborhood fast enough.

Grasping the envelope in her hand, she closed the door and locked it soundly behind her. Reading the note aloud, she sighed and tapped her smartwatch. With a feeling of impatience, she did the calculation in her head. One o'clock in the morning. Eight hours. What would she do with the longest eight hours of her life?

After pacing the floors until it became intolerable, Leah knew she had to try to settle herself down. Curled up in the corner of the couch trying to pay attention to yet another episode of Raymond, Leah was startled when the doorbell rang again. Looking at the clock, she saw it was only 8:00. Was this a change of plans? Pulling herself up from the couch she again quietly made her way to the door and peeked out. It was Daniel. Feeling like she saw an old friend even though she had just met him this morning, she was happy for the distraction.

Opening the door, she waved him in. "Hello, Daniel. I wasn't expecting to see you. How is your sister doing?"

As he stepped through the door, he lifted his hand to expose a beautiful bouquet of fresh flowers. "Hello, Leah. She is doing all right. The surgery was successful.

Thank you for asking." With some color rising to his face, he held the flowers out to her. "I wanted to give you these to show my appreciation for your help today."

"Thank you so much, but that wasn't necessary." Motioning to the kitchen, she added, "I'll just go put these in some water. They're lovely."

Following several steps behind her, he watched her dig through her cupboards to find a vase. Not finding one, she took out a glass pitcher and made due. With a look of guilt on her face, she said, "I still don't remember where I put everything from the move."

"I understand."

"Would you like some coffee? I can put on some decaf." Leah felt awkward with the situation.

"No, thank you," he replied.

Not sure what to say to add to the conversation, she was almost afraid to ask the question that was on her mind. "Did your mother say anything about her time with me today?"

He chuckled. "Not specifically but she seemed happy and quite exhausted."

With a quick thought, she provided part of an explanation. "We did go for a walk in the neighborhood."

Nodding his head with approval, Daniel said, "She does enjoy getting out for fresh air. Not so much for getting in the car though. That's part of why I didn't think it would be a good idea to take her along today. I hope it wasn't too much trouble to interrupt your day. I didn't mess up any plans you had, did I? I was desperate and I didn't think it through very well. I can't thank you enough for stepping up to help even though you don't know us. I knew the second you opened your door that you could be trusted and were a kind person. It shows in your eyes."

Not one for taking compliments very well, Leah waved it off. "It was no problem at all. Anyone would have done the same."

"Not true. Most people I know or meet wouldn't go out of their way at all to help someone in need. That's really a unique quality these days. Hard to find." His gaze rested on her flushed face.

Getting uncomfortable with the praise, she headed back to the front door hoping he would take the hint and leave. She opened the door and stood off to the side. "Thank you for the flowers."

"Absolutely." Reaching for the handle of the storm door, but before opening it, he turned to her and hesitated slightly before tilting his head just a touch to the side. Making eye contact, he asked, "Would you go out to dinner with me sometime?"

Averting her eyes, she asked with surprise, "Excuse me?"

Stammering slightly with embarrassment, Daniel shook his head slightly and self-consciously looked at her un-jeweled left hand with confusion. "Um. Would you..."

She cut him off before he could repeat the question. She held up her hand a bit and shook her head. "I'm sorry. I didn't mean to..."

This time he cut her off. He held up his hand to stop her. "I didn't mean to make this awkward. I just assumed. Not assumed, but um, sorry. I'll just go now before I dig myself deeper into this pit."

Relaxing a little knowing they were now on the same page, she chuckled. "It's complicated. Tell your mom I said good night. I'll see you."

"Yep. Night." Raising his hand up in a brief wave, he stepped outside and was quickly out of sight.

Closing the door and locking it behind her, she leaned against it and said out loud to the room, "That was weird."

Everyone was in their places. Most were unseen. The hour was arriving and it's what Agent Ryan and his team had been working on for years. They were so close. Adrenaline was coursing through everyone's veins. Nothing could get lost in the shuffle right now. Through his ear piece, he heard, "The flight has departed. Due to arrive at destination on time and on schedule."

"Copy that."

Looking at the wall clock then down to his cup of cold coffee, he knew there would be no hasty, rash decisions coming. Everything had been planned out in full detail with every possible distraction accounted for. Every possible contingency. But could you always know everything? It had to be perfect. There could be no mistakes. Not this time. Especially not this time.

With nervous anticipation, Leah left her house. Backing out of the driveway, she wondered how she would feel after the drop off and then returning to this house. Would she ever feel like she was living her real life again? Everything was so drastically different that it was hard to imagine. She was vacillating between nervous and curious excitement. Having always been one to only feel comfortable when in complete control of a situation, this was unusual. There were so many things that could go wrong. But yet, how wrong could they really go? She was afraid of Dale, but how far did that threat really go after he got what he wanted? She hadn't even opened her suitcase even though she had been intrigued about what was hiding in its depts. It obviously was something small. She didn't feel any additional weight to the bag. Knowing curiosity would only cause her trouble, she tried not to think about it.

The streets were deserted and dark. She noticed that several of the street lamps were burned out. Wondering whose job it was to have those replaced, her mind started formulating a plan to log all of the light poles and list the ones needing to be repaired. It was something concrete to have her mind fixed on in order to distract her from her current predicament. Her hands were starting to feel sweaty and clammy. She kept rubbing each one in turn down her pants legs. The memory of the kid's words when he handed her Dale's note were running through her mind. There was definitely something wrong with him. You could see it just by looking at him. His expression, his eyes, his stance. Defensive. Defiant. Determined. Dangerous. The fourth one kept her on her toes. Swallowing the lump in her throat, she continued the drive to the specified location. A dark, seemingly abandoned used car lot. From the looks of the dilapidated old building, it appeared to have been neglected for quite some time. Several windows were broken. None of the surrounding lights were working. It was on the edge of town and there was nothing else around for a least a block in each direction. He had chosen a perfect location.

Leah saw his shadow lurking in the driver's seat of the only vehicle parked in the large, desolate lot. Realizing the seriousness of her situation, she stopped her car several yards away from his. She jumped out and grabbed the suitcase from the back seat. Rolling it towards him, she was about to jump back into her own vehicle when he barked out. "No. Bring it to me."

She shook her head. "No need. Whatever you want is in there. I never even opened it up. I swear."

"I don't believe you. Bring it here." His voice demanded compliance.

Leah wheeled it several more feet in his direction then pushed it forward with her foot. She took several steps backward toward her car.

"Don't move." He stepped closer and reached for the suitcase. Opening the zipper, he reached inside and a slow smile spread across his face. "Good." Then he held out his hand toward her. "Come on, now. Let's go. I have everything ready for us."

Fear etched across her features. She stepped further away. "I don't know what you mean. I brought what you wanted."

"You did. What's in that suitcase will give us the life we deserve. I already found a house for us. It's perfect. Just you and me."

With trembling hands and a shaky voice, she said, "No. I don't even know you."

"You will. You're part of the plan." He smiled at her with a look in his eyes that she had never seen before. It chilled her to the bone. "I picked you. Of all the people at the airport, I chose you. You are so lucky." He stared at

134

her as if waiting for a reply. "Aren't you going to say something?"

"I don't know what you mean." Leah was looking around for a way to escape. She could make it to her car but probably not get in and get the doors locked before he reached her.

"Aren't you going to thank me?"

"Thank you for what?" Leah could feel blood coursing through her ears. Everything turned muted and dull. Physically shaking her head in an effort to clear it, she looked at him with confusion and terror unmistakable in her expression.

Although he was thrilled to see her fear, he didn't have time for her to be disagreeable. Anger flashed across his face as his voice rose. "Aren't you going to thank me for making you part of my plan? You get to ride off my success. Aren't you grateful?" He took a heavy step forward.

Sucking in her breath, she tried to think fast. "Of course. Thank you, Dale. For making me part of your plan."

His eyes narrowed. "How did you know my name was Dale?" He looked around him with suspicion.

She answered calmly, "I heard the police call you that when they had you on the ground at the airport. They let me walk right past. They had no idea I was part of your plan, did they?" She hoped she didn't sound patronizing.

With a slightly noticeable puff to his chest, he replied, "No. They had no idea. I'm always one step ahead of those morons." Reaching out to her, he waved her over. "Come on, let's go before someone sees us. Just leave your car here."

"No. I don't think that's a good idea. You should go alone. I would just slow you down. They might start looking for me." She tried to stall so she could think of an escape.

He clenched his jaw and balled his hands into fists. "Does this have to do with the man who brought you flowers tonight?"

"What?" It almost made her want to throw up thinking he had been watching her.

"You won't come with me because you had someone over tonight? They don't matter. It's just you and me now. Let's go."

She shook her head and turned to run the opposite direction from where he was standing. She didn't know where she was going to run but anywhere away from him would work. She had hardly made it 20 feet before she could feel his hand grab a tight hold of her arm. He jerked her to a stop. "This can go easy or hard. Your choice."

Just as he was about to start dragging her toward his car, headlights shined in their direction.

Dale cursed under his breath.

Loud rock music poured out from the car which had several people inside. The vibrations from the bass could be felt in her bones. The car slowed and Leah took advantage of the distraction to pull her arm from his grip. She ran to her car and slid behind the wheel. Taking off toward her house, she tried to stop her hands from shaking. Moving her arm around, she could almost feel the bruise starting to take shape where his fingers had clamped onto her flesh. The car had come by right at a perfect time. What would have been the outcome if she hadn't been able to escape Dale's grip? The thought made her scalp tingle with sweat. Pulling into her garage with the suitcase handed over, she had expected to feel relief. Instead, she felt a jittery nauseousness that made her mouth water. She kept telling herself, 'It's over. It's over.' If only she could truly believe it.

Chapter 10

Dale was fuming. It was a good thing his days of doing this kind of work were almost over. It seemed that nothing went quite right for him anymore. One final payday and he wouldn't have to worry about it. This woman was becoming such a nuisance that she hardly seemed worth it. He would have to decide if she was going to still be part of his plan or maybe he would find someone different on the trip to his new house. Someone who wasn't such a problem. He hated changing plans. He would have to think long and hard about it. Although if he were being honest with himself, he had already started obsessing over her so the chances of changing his mind were pretty slim. Her timid demeanor was what drew her to him from the beginning. He was really surprised to see how much fight she actually had in her. He enjoyed a challenge. He could break her fighting spirit. It would actually be a pleasure. Not sure what to do with all of his pent-up energy, he just drove around being careful not to break any speeding or traffic laws. He couldn't allow any other glitches in his night.

Walking into the house should have been comforting. However, she actually felt more nervous than she had before she had left to meet Dale. She quickly went from door to door and window to window to verify that they were securely locked. She turned on all of the outside lights and most of the ones inside also. Collapsing on the couch, she tried to concentrate on breathing. Simply in and out. Slowly. Leah almost instantly fell asleep after the long day of crazy surprises. She was absolutely worn out. Quickly heading for deep sleep after the ordeals leading up to this night, she found herself in a dream that felt as real as if she were right in the middle of it.

Leah was walking through the deserted airport. Confusion spread all over her as she looked for the way out or for someone to give her directions towards the exit. It felt like she had been walking for miles. Her body was heavy with exhaustion and her left arm had a weighted sleeve from her wrist to her elbow. It was aching and throbbing. Her surroundings were completely quiet. No overhead speakers loudly announcing flight arrivals or departures or boarding information. No TVs blaring and no screaming children running around the terminal. She was just about ready to give up and sit for a rest when she spotted someone ahead of her. Calling out to them, she hollered into the silence, "Hello? Can you help me?" As she got closer to the individual, she realized with horror that it was Dale.

Turning around she started running down the empty corridor. She couldn't tell if he was chasing her or not but she didn't dare turn around to check. It seemed as if she started running slower and slower. She could suddenly hear footsteps close behind her. "Leah." Dale's voice said almost in her ear, "Leah. Come with me."

She kept trying to run but she felt as if her legs had turned to rubber. They were hard to move and she struggled to even stay upright. Up ahead she could make out the outline of a door leading outside. Trying to look out the window as she ran, it looked dark and deserted. Maybe there was someone out there that could help her. She hadn't seen anyone inside yet, so her hope was quickly wavering for help indoors. Hopefully there were workers still outside that would come to her aid. She veered to the right and headed to the door. She could feel Dale breathing on the back of her hair. "Leah."

With a quick burst of speed, she made her way out the door and across the tarmac. She ran and ran and no one came into sight. It was only darkness and her labored breathing. Eventually, she saw a light up ahead. Not hearing footsteps behind her, she ran to the light. Someone must be out here. As she got closer, she made out the lines of an airplane with steps leading down to the pavement. She thought she could see a person in the cockpit. Hollering with what little breath she had left, she cried out, "Help. Help me, please!"

As she got close to the steps, the runway guard lights lit up and started flashing. The plane's engine roared to a start and shook the ground. Making a last-ditch effort to reach the bottom step, she grabbed the handrail and ran up the steps. The more steps she took, the further away the door was. The engine got louder and the steps started moving away from the opening. Taking what little breath was left in her, she focused on the lighted access to her only source of help and with sheer determination, she started making progress toward the top. The stairs were getting farther away and she had to make a split- second decision when she reached the top. Not knowing if Dale was still behind her or not, she didn't dare take the chance he might be. Lunging the full force of her body toward the doorway, she threw herself into its lighted opening.

Taking a few seconds to catch her breath, she quickly observed her surroundings. The floor's edge

143

lights dimly illuminated the narrow path to the rear of the vessel. Listening closely, she heard movements in the cockpit. "Hello! Can you help me?" Leah hollered as loud as her hoarse voice would allow. She was so winded from running that she could hardly function. Getting to her knees, she used the wall to help her stand up. Pounding on the door to the cockpit, she waited for an answer. She lost her breath all together when the response to her pounding was a gentle knock from the other side. "Leah. Come with me." Turning around to quickly exit the plane, she remembered the stairs had been moving away. Sure enough, they were gone. Nothing but enveloping darkness greeted her. As dark as a cave five miles in. Hearing the handle of the cockpit door moving, she ran toward the back of the plane. All of the lights went off and she was shrouded in a complete blanket of cover. No shadows. No dusk. She lost all track of direction. Feeling around her, she touched the top of a seat. Hearing the door creak at the front of the plane, she did the only thing she could think of. She stepped up onto the arm of the

144

seat, opened the overhead compartment, stepped onto the headrest of the seat, and pulled herself into the compartment. Reaching out from her hiding place, she tried to locate to door to close around her. She pulled it hard, slamming it closed at the same time the cockpit door crashed open.

"Leah. Why are you hiding from me? I have plans for us. You're coming with me." She shuddered at his voice. He was still a little way off but she could hear his voice clearly. Her heart was already pounding against her ribs. She felt like he would be able to hear her heavy breathing and tried to calm herself. Shaking with fear, she tried to formulate a plan. Trapped in the compartment, she had no escape route. Her blood ran cold when she heard the first compartment door being opened. "Leah. Are you playing a game with me? I have time. We have the rest of your life to be together." He spoke with a calmness that scared her. One by one, she heard to doors opening up and with each sound, his voice came closer. It sounded every bit as evil as the penetrating, knife-

stabbing look in his eyes had been earlier when he tried to

take her. It felt like a second and yet a day when she could

hear him outside her compartment. "Leah. Let's go."

  She held her breath and shrunk as far back into

the tiny area as she could. He opened the door and the

darkness was suddenly lit by the floor runner lights

popping on again. It left him in a menacing shadow of

wickedness. He smiled at her but the smile didn't reach

his eyes. They bore through her and she could feel the evil

radiating from him.

  "My name is not Leah!" She yelled, as she pulled

away from his reaching grab.

  Pulling as far as she could back into the cold,

cramped space, she was determined to fight with

everything in her. There was no way she was going with

him. He grabbed her by her arm and was about to pull her

out when she leaned back with all her might to release his

grip. The back of the compartment opened up into the still

night air and she screamed as she fell from the back of the

chamber toward the ground. With legs and arms flailing,
she was certain she was about to die.

With a jump and a scream, Leah startled herself awake. She was trembling and gasping. Feeling like she might start to cry, she got up on shaky legs and made her way to the kitchen for a glass of water. Shaking her head to clear the awful thoughts from the nightmare, she hoped it would be a dream she would forget quickly like most dreams whether good or bad. Taking note of the time on the microwave, she felt a tiny bit calmer as she did quick math.

After pacing for several minutes, Leah decided to go try to get some real sleep in bed. Trying to convince herself that couch dreams were often worse than bed dreams, she knew she would not likely fall asleep again this night. As she walked past the front door heading to the bedroom, she heard a noise outside. Knowing she was just feeling jittery, she thought about ignoring it. She could hear a voice in her head. "Look for me in the shadows." Out loud, she stated, "I feel you. Stay with me."

Leah climbed into bed feeling like her limbs were heavy weights. Her body felt like it had been through a battle. Breathing slowly through her nose and trying to clear her mind and relax her muscles, she started melting into the mattress. With a big sigh of comfort, she felt like she was at a turning point. Feeling like she might actually be able to sleep, she was calmly listening to the quiet around her. Just before dozing off, she heard what sounded like a quiet knock. Was that the front door? Maybe she had already started to dream again. Trying once more to doze, the knock was louder this time and it startled her into full alertness. There was no way it could be Dale. He wouldn't have the nerve to come here again after getting spooked a second time. Would he? He had what he wanted. Why didn't he just go away now?

With a feeling of dread slowly creeping through her, she realized with horror that maybe what was in the suitcase wasn't all he wanted. Maybe his threats of taking her were real. The nightmare she recently woke from ran in circles through her mind. She crawled back out from

148

the covers and slinked her way down the hall toward the door. Sneaking toward the tiny glass hole to take a peek, she almost screamed out loud when the quiet knock sounded again. Jumping enough to make a noise, she took the several steps forward to finally take the dreaded look at her visitor. Wrinkling her brow in confusion, she was surprised to see not only that it wasn't Dale, but that it was nobody. Feeling like she might be losing her mind, she stood still for several minutes not sure what to do. There was a rustling outside. With fear rising again, Leah called out in what she hoped was a firm voice, "Who's there?"

A quiet, tired, woman's voice asked, "John?"

Opening the door without even thinking about it, Leah gasped when she saw Elinore sitting on the landing outside the door and leaning against it so Leah couldn't open it to reach her. "Elinore?" Leah called loudly. "Elinore, I can't get to you."

Elinore turned her head in Leah's direction and Leah could see that her friend had been crying. "John? Where is John?"

149

Leah could tell that Elinore didn't recognize her. She ran to the kitchen and grabbed her cell phone from her purse. Calling the number Daniel had given her earlier, she waited impatiently for him to answer.

"Hello?" Daniel answered in a still half sleeping voice.

"Daniel, it's Leah."

Sounding much more awake, Daniel responded, "Yea. Leah. Everything all right?"

Knowing it must be extremely confusing and contradictory to their previous conversation, she quickly explained her call. "Your mom is here outside my front door. She's asking for John and I can't get out to her. I'm going to go out through the garage door but I don't know what to do."

"I'll head right over. Thank you for calling me. Apparently, the aide on night duty isn't at the top of her game. I'll call her on my way." Daniel sounded frazzled and Leah didn't blame him at all. She wondered how often this type of event happened. It was heartbreaking really.

Opening the garage door, she rounded the side of the house to get to Elinore on the front step. The elderly woman recoiled from Leah as she came near. She looked at Leah with fear in her eyes.

Not getting too close, Leah sat on the second step and asked in a quiet voice, "Elinore. It's your neighbor, Leah. Are you okay?" She could see the woman's eyes darting around trying to make out where she was. The light from inside the house was coming out the storm door but it didn't shine very far.

"Why am I outside in the dark of night?" she asked.

"I think you just wandered over to say hello. Let's go inside until Daniel gets here." She got up and reached over to help Elinore up. Taking the woman's arm, she gently led her around the side of the house. As they neared the garage, a car drove into the driveway. Not knowing how far away Daniel was coming from, she was skeptical that it was him already. Trying not to let fear drive her thoughts, she looked around for something to use as a weapon if necessary. Hearing the car door open, she turned in the direction of the car and as the headlights turned off and the interior light shined, she saw that it was, in fact, Daniel. With a big sigh of relief, she continued to lead Elinore into the house.

"Will you close the garage door behind you, Daniel?" she asked even though she knew it would most likely be only for a few minutes. No use asking for trouble.

As Leah helped Elinore take a seat at the table, Daniel followed and knelt in front of his mom. "Are you ok, mom?" He gently took her hand in his and stroked if softly.

Elinore just stared at him as if she hadn't heard the question. Shoulders slumping, he let go of her hand, got up and took several steps into the kitchen to have a quiet conversation with Leah.

"She is getting worse every day. We've been trying to keep her at home but obviously we have to get her someplace safer. I was hoping her familiar surroundings would be beneficial but this can't happen

152

again. What if you weren't here or didn't hear her. She might have sat outside all night. I'm so sorry I've brought so much complication into your life."

Leah smiled a tiny smile before answering, "I'm glad I was here to help. Believe it or not, I needed the distraction. No need to apologize."

"If you consider this just a distraction, I'm afraid your life must indeed be very complicated." Daniel tried to make a joke of it but it fell flat. He could see the look of concern on her face. "Leah, are you ok? You look like you've seen a ghost."

With a soft chuckle, she said, "Yes. I'm ok. And yes, my life is very complicated. But it's about to become less so."

"I'll do my part." With a nod of appreciation he asked, "Is it all right if I leave my car here while I walk my mom back home? I'll make sure the aide is actually awake and stays awake."

"Of course." With that, Leah walked them to the front door.

Turning back to her, Daniel asked with concern, "Are you sure you're ok? Is there something I can help you with?"

"I'm sure. Thank you for the offer but I'm fine." Nodding with a forced smile on her face, she shooed him out the door.

Knowing with complete certainty that she was not going to be able to sleep tonight, she grabbed a book and curled up in the corner of the couch. It was going to be a long wait for the sun to show itself.

Chapter 11

Dale drove slowly past and felt anger rising at the sight of a car in his wife's driveway. He could tell there was a light on in the house. He considered at the very least slashing the car's tires but that would just prevent the person from eventually leaving. This would definitely get in the way of him sneaking around to find a way inside. He was supposed to meet his boss at 8:00 to get his money. That wasn't going to leave much time for him to come back and get her before heading out of town. She was already delaying his plans. She was going to have to learn that it was not acceptable to get in the way of his plans. He worked hard to make sure his plans always came together one way or another. He was losing patience with her.

At least the police weren't here. She must not have called them. His threatening note had apparently worked. He had worded it nicely for her and wondered if she noticed how neat he made his penmanship so she was sure to understand the meaning of everything. Now he wouldn't have to worry about the police searching for his car. As far as the car in the driveway, Dale felt confident that he could handle any obstacle that got in his way. He caressed the handle of the knife that laid on the seat next to him. He actually relished the idea of using it again. Not wanting to get too distracted with additional plans, he continued on his way while keeping it open as an option if need be.

Heading back to the motel, Dale thought he might be able to get a little rest before the new day dawned. Reaching into his pocket, he pulled out the container of pills. Popping off the lid, he tipped one into his hand and threw it into the back of his mouth. Out of instant reflex his throat contracted around it without the help of any liquid. Putting the lid back on, he shook the bottle. Had he been taking more than usual? He shouldn't be almost out already. If his boss wanted to get the information tomorrow, he might have to provide more of these pills. Dale held all the cards in this game. Maybe he shouldn't have agreed to the amount of payment. This information was almost priceless. Not only the information in the suitcase that now rode in the trunk of his car, but also the information that was in his memory. Names, places, dates. He had a lot of it stored in his mind for future use if necessary. He tried to recall some of it from the beginning of his career and was surprised to realize that he was getting foggy with the recollection. Trying to convince himself that it was just because he was tired, he pulled into the parking spot in front of his room at the motel.

Getting out of the car and drawing in a deep breath of the fresh air around him, he decided to take a short stroll around the lot before heading to bed. Maybe it would clear some of the cobwebs from his mind. As he crossed the way, he heard a dog barking. That's probably the same stupid dog that woke him up this morning. Annoyed at the attention it might draw to him, he turned to go back in the direction of his room.

157

Around the corner, the dog came charging toward him. Not one for friendly interaction with his K-9 foe, he turned back to shush the dog when a sharp pain in his hand made him cry out. Instinct made him pull his hand away from the source of the pain before he realized the dog's mouth was clamped onto it. With a swift kick, he sent the dog flying several feet. Luckily the dog took off back to where it belonged but now Dale was left with a bite that was bleeding and extremely painful. Well, he certainly couldn't go to the hospital to get it looked at. He wasn't about to start answering questions. With disgust and curses, he stormed into his room and did what he could to wash it out. The useless, miniscule bar of hotel soap didn't even produce a lather. Well, it had to be better than nothing. Cutting the bottom of the sheet with his knife to give him something to try to wrap it with, his heart pounded with pain and anger. He did the best he could with only one hand. This entire job was getting too costly for him. Someone was going to have to pay. Maybe everyone.

Leah had read the same page of her book three times before she gave up and laid it on the coffee table. Time stood still. It was the quiet of pre-dawn. Nothing made noise. All was completely silent. Except of course the ticking of the clock on the wall. Leah loved the sound. It reminded her that even though time felt like it was standing still, the minutes were still marching on. Looking out the kitchen window, she stared into the darkness. What was happening right now? Soon, the birds would be out singing their wake-up songs, buses would be taking children to school, people would be dressing for work and businesses would be opening their doors. But how would her day go? How does a day seem normal after what she had just been through? She thought about Elinore and wondered if she felt this lost every day? Right now, at this minute, nothing moved. Nothing and seemingly no one else in the world was awake. Just her and her thoughts.

Feeling trapped in the confines of the walls surrounding her, she wondered if this was what prison felt like? She didn't feel the luxury of the freedom of just leaving the house. It was one thing to choose to stay home. Entirely another to have the choice of staying taken away. Dale might still be around. She couldn't chance his unhinged thoughts that may or may not still include her. That was a bizarre twist out of left field that she had never expected. She paced the small space between rooms in the house. She went in and took a shower long enough to run the hot water completely cold.

Dale had not done well with the limited time he had before meeting his boss. His dog-bitten hand had turned red halfway up to his elbow and he felt the swollen tenderness of it under the dirty knot of the bunched-up sheet. He had taken the last of the pills from his container and they did nothing except make his mind foggy. They didn't help at all with the pain. Sitting at the small desk, he rocked back and forth staring into the hazy, damp air of his room. He didn't know why it seemed hazy. The dull, low-watt light bulb was probably meant to hide some of the more unsatisfactory touches in the room. But it shouldn't seem so gloomy. He didn't smoke and he couldn't smell anything burning. Annoyed that there wasn't a coffee pot in his room, he decided to venture out to the front desk area and see if they had a community pot out there. If so, hopefully it was fresh instead of stale and cold from yesterday.

The desk clerk looked warily at him as he entered the small lobby area. Looking at Dale's wrapped hand and sweaty, pale face, he knew better than to ask any questions. People who stayed in this place usually didn't want to be asked personal questions. "Morning. What can I do for you?" the clerk asked with as much pleasantness as he could muster.

With a slight slur and unfocused eyes, Dale answered, "You got any fresh coffee around here?"

"I usually make some in about an hour but I'd be happy to brew you up a pot now if you'd like," the clerk answered with false cheerfulness. He didn't really like this job and liked the guests even less but he needed it as a second income to help pay some of his expenses.

"Yep."

"Ok." He walked over to the counter that had the remains of yesterday's coffee still in its dirty pot. He dumped the thick, black liquid into the adjoining sink and didn't even rinse it out. He filled it with water from the tap and poured the scummy-looking water into the back of the outdated coffeemaker.

Dale got tired of watching the process and went outside into the stillness of the chilly, morning air. He sat outside the door in an old fold-up lawn chair with a sagging seat. The chill was clearing his head a little and he started planning the next few hours. Just one more day. Tomorrow he would wake up in his new location and finally be living his dream. That brought him again to the woman. It wouldn't be quite the same now if he had to start his new life alone. He should never have allowed her to be part of his plan. But now that she was part of it, he had to follow through with it. He would get his money then go to her. This time he wouldn't be as courteous in explaining it to her.

The clerk opened the door and told him the coffee was ready whenever he wanted it.

Walking back to his room with the steaming, burnt-tasting coffee, he was starting to feel more aware. The fog from his mind was clearing. Along with it came pain shooting through his hand. He would make one stop on his way to get his money. He would get a few things from the pharmacy for pain and to properly wrap his wound. No sense letting it get infected. That could put his plans in jeopardy. And there was no way he would allow anyone to jeopardize his plans at this point. Not even himself.

Agent Ryan had not slept in days. Timing was everything and it appeared that everyone was ready. It could be any time. Communication was key and each person involved was at the top of their game. They had been closing in on Dale and his leader for over a year. Instead of just getting

Dale, they wanted to get the guy in charge. The guy issuing the orders. And most importantly make sure to stop the trafficking in its tracks. It was just one of so many cases but to stop one at a time was necessary in order to rid all of it. They had to do everything right. Somehow the criminals knew every possible way to get out of responsibility. The so-called "get out of jail free card". Agent Ryan and his agency had crossed all their T's and dotted all of their I's. There was no doubt that they had everything needed for prosecution. All they had to do to finish the task was follow Dale to his boss's location and get the suitcase with all of the information.

They had noticed Dale becoming more and more distracted and disturbed the past few days. That seemed to some like a good thing but those closely involved knew how dangerous that could become. Dale felt like he had nothing to lose at this point. He had been distracted from his mission twice now which they knew was making him more unstable. Witnessing the dog bite several hours ago, they knew he would be even more unpredictable. Things weren't going his way and Dale was vicious when he lost control. They had witnessed it in the past but had never had enough proof to put him behind bars for any length of time.

Over the headset, Agent Ryan heard the code. "The flight has departed. All crew is on board."

With his heart beating hard enough to be felt externally, Agent Ryan had never felt fear like he did on this mission. He would wait for the final confirmation of landing before he left the building.

Chapter 12

Mari sat curled up in the corner of the dark, musty pit. Keeping track of the number of days in her head originally seemed like a good idea, but as days kept being added, she thought it might have been better not to keep track. It was now 74 days since she had been taken. Her thoughts went for the thousandth time to that fateful day. Leaving work later than usual, she had been ridiculously tired and completely not paying attention. If she had been at the top of her game, she might have noticed the vehicle following her. Or heard the van door sliding open when she got out of her car to go into her apartment. They grabbed her so quickly that she was almost certain no one probably even noticed it. As far as she knew, the cameras in the parking lot had not been actively working since she had moved in several years ago.

Boredom and fear were her constant companions. At first, she was afraid to lean up against the wall because the bugs would crawl on her and she had received a bite of some kind from every conceivable insect making its home in the small dirt room. Now she didn't care. The first time a gecko had squeezed its way through the opening overhead, and crawled down the wall to investigate her, she screamed at the feel of it running over her leg. However, she quickly got used to the curious little creature and she now called him "friend". She didn't know what to name him so that seemed as good a name as any. He was in fact the only friend she currently had. No one even knew where she was and she assumed no one probably cared.

The only thing that helped at all was that several weeks into her detention, the usual guy who came to bring her food and water didn't show up and in his place was a younger man who was much friendlier. He said his name was Evan, but she didn't know if that was his real name or not. It took some time to build trust between each other.

Eventually she learned that her brother had not fulfilled his delivery of promised inventory and they had taken her to ensure that he would follow through with his commitment. It was hard to know how to feel about that information. Mari knew her brother had gotten mixed up with some bad things but never would she have believed it was serious enough to involve family members being taken. She didn't know if she would be considered kidnapped or some type of hostage. Either way, the end result wasn't looking good.

When Evan showed up, he brought with him music. Not from a radio or phone but from his lungs. He could sing like nobody else she had ever heard. He would take requests from her or he would sing songs she had never heard before. He stayed longer than he should and she was always afraid the others would get mad and not let him come any more. It was Evan who snuck her a blanket and pillow. That first night was a dream with a pillow. She never realized how many things she took for granted each day.

He would bring her food and water but also, he would regularly sneak her some extra. Sometimes it was gum or candy. Once it was a small bag of beef jerky. She had been very thoughtful about rationing out a little each day. It gave her something to look forward to. But the best gift of all had been a small pen light. She was afraid to use it very often for fear of it dying. It was just enough light to shine her way into familiarity with her surroundings. She had dug a small hole in the corner where she hid her few special belongings.

There was no way for her to get out or anyone else to get in. Her food and water were sent down about 15 feet from a hinged rickety door located in the ceiling. It was a rigged little rustic tray with a rope around each side. It reminded her of an old tree swing that had been tied together where you would place your hands to lean back and make the swing go higher and higher. She remembered days when she and her brother would go to the playground at the abandoned old school house. They would have a contest to see who could go higher and then who could jump the farthest off the swing. She could still see the sky overhead in her imagination from when she would tilt back to watch the clouds scurry across the blue openness. Her long hair would touch the ground and she would have the dust and dirt from the dry surface in her hair until it was washed out down the drain later that night before bed. What she wouldn't give to see that sky right now.

The problem currently was that she was losing hope. She had been filled with it in the beginning. Mari had a feeling that if their intention had been to kill her, they would have already done so.

She had started to crave Evan's visits. Not just for the food but for the companionship and conversation. The gift of exchanged words. Evan would open the trap door and lower down the food. He would sit with his feet dangling over the edge while they would talk or he would sing. He never said much about himself but would ask about her and they would talk about the weather and sports and news. Today he seemed a little quieter than usual. "I brought you something I think you will like." Evan called down into the darkness.

"Really?" Mari asked with excitement. "What is it?"

Evan sent down the tray with something bigger than usual on it. As it arrived, Mari sucked in her breath. She slowly removed the precious gift from its carrier. She could make out the cover of the book in the light shining from the opening where Evan sat. "That's amazing. Thank you so much!" She looked up and Evan could see the happiness in her eyes but it didn't reach her mouth. He had never seen her smile. He imagined she had a beautiful smile. He didn't want to tell her that he had been trying to come up with a plan to get her out of here. If he wasn't careful, it could get them both killed so he was taking his time and gathering what was needed for them to just disappear from the area. Not knowing for sure if she would even want to go with him, he figured he would take his chances.

Lately Evan had been feeling more tension than usual around the people he worked with. He felt that something was about to go down. He didn't want to chance something happening to him and then Mari might be left here with no one to really care about her. He had realized with surprise several weeks ago that he had grown to really care about Mari and he loved the small amount of time he got to spend with her. What a crazy situation. Maybe someday they would laugh about the circumstances that brought them together but it certainly would take a while. He didn't know if she would ditch him as soon as he helped her escape. After all, he was part of the group that kept her detained. She couldn't know that he was as much their prisoner as she was. His own brother was also the one of the guilty parties keeping him chained to the group's will. At least he and Mari had that in common. Their brothers had made some bad choices. Evan had finally concluded that he and Mari had paid enough for their brother's indiscretions. It was time they paid their own consequences and he and Mari could move past it.

Responding to Mari's appreciation for the book, he answered. "You're welcome. Go ahead and use your flashlight as much as you want. I can get you another one if it runs out."

"This is going to help pass the time so much easier. I can't thank you enough."

"Mari, I have to ask you a question."

"Ok."

"Do you trust me?"

The question took her by surprise and at first, she didn't answer. She had been let down by so many people in her life. Evan was one of the few people who she actually felt comfortable around. That sounded strange even to her since she was completely at his mercy in this situation. Looking up to the young man staring down at her with a look of great expectation in his eyes as he waited for her answer, she slowly nodded her head. "I do."

With a smile that she could clearly see, he let out the breath he hadn't realized he was holding. "Good. I promise I won't let you down."

Mari looked up at him with a hope she hadn't felt in a long time. Maybe things were finally about to change. At least there was finally a possibility. And where there was possibility, anything could happen.

Dale packed what few belongings he had left scattered throughout the motel room. Not even glancing back, he slammed the door behind him hoping to maybe wake someone up from a good sleep. He had hoped to be in a good mood since this was finally the time to start his new life but he only found himself feeling irritable and uncomfortable. The nasty coffee had upset his stomach and his nerves were starting to get jumpy since he knew he was out of his pills. Trying to calm himself down, he made an effort to follow all traffic laws as he made his way to the pharmacy. He was starting to feel like this was his home away from home. Not that he had a home right now.

He slipped into the emptiness of the store without being noticed. This time of day, no one was really out yet. He found the aisle with pain killers and grabbed the biggest bottle of the strongest one available. Adding some large bandages along with antibiotic ointment, he made his way to the front of the store. Deciding to grab an energy drink to wash his medicine down, he had his hands full as he made his way to the counter. Half way there he dropped the bandages. Feeling his anger start to rise, he cursed under his breath. He wanted to scream and throw his drink through the glass door at the entrance but at that moment the door opened and someone else entered the store. Not wanting to draw attention to himself, he walked to the counter and set his items down before walking back to get the bandages from the floor.

Using all of his patience, he paid for his purchases and made it out to the car before exploding. He cursed and ranted and raved and yelled until he almost felt tired. With his hand swollen and aching, he had a hard time opening the bottle of pain killers. Finally getting it open, he poured some into his hand and threw them into his mouth. They sat on his tongue getting pasty as he struggled to open the energy drink. Downing half of its contents in an attempt to get the chalky taste from his mouth, he leaned his head back against the head rest and tried to calm himself. He pulled the temporary sheet-bandage from his hand and threw it onto the floor of the passenger side. Having trouble again with packaging, he was cursing by the time he had squeezed too much ointment onto the wound and found that the bandage wouldn't stick. Throwing the bandage onto the seat, he reached across the seat and grabbed the bloody sheet section and used it to wipe some of the antibiotic off. Trying again with success this time, he covered the bite and turned on the car. Looking at the dash board clock, he realized he didn't have much time to spare so he quickly began his short journey to the meeting place. As angry and out of control as he could get, he knew that Big Fish could get ten times worse. Wade Fisher had a reputation for violence and Dale didn't want to be on the wrong end of one of his bad days.

Arriving at the giant warehouse, he drove around to the back. The front part was still in use and there were people milling about but once he got to the described section of the building, it was as if he were in a different location. Stepping from his car, he noticed an eerie stillness in the air. It felt as if all life refused to be in the vicinity. No sounds of vehicles, birds, voices, anything. This was perfect. Dale grabbed the suitcase by its handle from the back seat and walked to the building. He opened the heavy door leading to some vacant offices and made his way down the hall to the last door on the left. It was dark and musty smelling in the closed-up building.

As he entered the room, Dale took a deep breath to try to calm himself. Wade, known to Dale only as "Big Fish", was sitting at a worn-out conference table with the overhead lights flickering every so often. Even though he had just come into the room, the flickering was already starting to make him jittery. Walking to the table, Dale

178

dropped the suitcase to the floor before pulling a chair away from the table with his foot. The suitcase rolled several feet away before falling onto its side.

Wade nodded toward Dale. He looked Dale up and down with his eyes, eventually ending up staring at his swollen, bandaged hand for several seconds before shaking his head. "Looks like you been through the ringer."

"Yep." Dale snapped at him. He knew he was on touchy ground, but he was agitated and couldn't help it.

"No one followed you?"

"Nope."

"You sure?"

Dale glared a glassy stare at his boss. "Yes. I'm sure. Have I ever been followed before?" He kicked the suitcase with his foot and sent it several more feet away from him. "I got your stuff so let's settle up so I can get outta here."

Wade noticed the sweat pouring off of Dale in the damp, chilly room. Squinting at him with scrutiny, Wade

179

asked without the slightest compassion in his voice, "What's wrong with you?"

"Nothing. Where's my money? And I need more pills. You got some with you?" Dale tried not to sound desperate.

"You stupid fool. I provided you plenty three days ago. You didn't take all of them already, did you?" He started looking around nervously. "You know what happens when you take too much of that?" He stood up abruptly and his chair slid across the floor and banged into the wall. "You make mistakes!" He shouted at him. Leaning down and placing his fisted-up hands onto the table top, he leaned over and spoke with contempt, "You are worthless baggage. You know that? This was going to be your last job because you are getting sloppy and stupid. I should have known better than to think you were up to it."

Dale felt fire burning inside his hand, face and chest. He stood up and yelled back, "I got your stuff. It's in the pocket of the bag. I did my job. Now pay me so I can get going."

Wade went to the bag and opened it up. He retrieved the information and put it into the case he had laying on the table. He pulled out an envelope and dumped it onto the table. It had stacks of money and an ID.

Dale pulled the ID from the pile and felt bile rise up in his throat. "You gave me his name? How dare you!" The ID read Foster Smith. Foster was the name of Dale's best friend who had been killed by Wade when he didn't follow through with a job. He was the only person who Dale had ever trusted and they had been like brothers. Dale lunged across the table at Wade but in his unstable condition, Wade just grabbed him by the shirt and pulled him the rest of the way across the table and threw him onto the floor.

Wade pulled his gun from the back of his waistband and pointed it at Dale's head. "You have become a liability to me." With disgust he took several slow breaths. "You know I almost feel sorry for you. Almost. No one will even notice you're gone. No one will miss you. No one will look for you."

Dale felt powerful all of a sudden. He was still fuzzy in his thoughts but having a gun pointed at his head suddenly helped him think more clearly. He didn't know if it would work or not but it was worth a try. "If I don't show up at my location by six o'clock tonight, I have someone mailing the information to the coppers. They will find you in no time." He sneered a creepy snarl at Wade and challenged him with a stare.

Wade didn't believe him. Lifting the gun, he leaned over, smacking Dale in the temple.

Dale didn't even feel the blood run down the side of his head.

"It's encrypted and you are way too dumb to figure it out. Why do you think I chose you for the job?"

Dale smiled at him. "I may not be bright enough to figure out your wacko encryption but I remember things. I remember names. Places. Dates and times. I've been keeping track of them for a long time. From the beginning, pal."

Wade laughed almost uncontrollably. Standing to his full height in order to tower over his bleeding informant, he kicked Dale in the ribs several times before reaching down to grab his shirt. He forcefully pulled Dale up to as much of a standing position as was possible with the wind knocked out of him. Wade shoved him toward the door with the gun dug into his back. "Then I guess we're going for a ride."

Dale's thoughts were muddled. He knew he had to think fast but he also knew that wasn't going to happen. He was past the point of being angry and knew he was at the mercy of Big Fish. That was not a good place to be. How did this happen? He had no plan. He had not prepared for anything but success. He also knew that he had nothing to lose at this point. Using what little awareness he possessed; he did the only thing he knew how to do.

Wade was shoving the gun into Dale's back leading him to the SUV parked at the edge of the building. Dale tripped and fell to the ground. He mumbled and tried to get up. Falling back to the dirt parking lot, he stayed on the ground muttering and mumbling to himself.

Wade pulled him by the shirt. "Get up you idiot!" He pulled him to a semi-standing position before leading him along again. "How much of that stuff did you take? It can kill you; you know."

Using all of his strength, Dale whipped around and knocked the gun from Wade's hand. "I know!" he hollered. Dale also knew it would be a short battle. He had everything going against him right now. Injuries, medication, legal and illegal. Dale got in one good punch before Wade's fist connected with Dale's jaw and dropped him to his knees. Reaching for his gun, Wade stopped in his tracks as he noticed multiple red dots pointed at his chest.

From out of nowhere, from every direction, the flurry began. "Hands up! Get on the ground! Don't reach for it!"

Dale was almost completely out of it when they handcuffed him. The good news was that they couldn't pin this on him. He didn't have possession of the information. Sometimes luck just played in your favor.

Mari leaned against the cold dirt wall. She didn't know if anyone had ever given her something so valuable. She ran her finger down the spine of the book. Holding it up to her nose, she inhaled the scent of worn paper. Finally, there was a way to escape this nightmare she was living. Even if it was only through the pages of a story, she would have a distraction. Something to take her mind off of what was now called her life. Turning on the tiny light, she opened to the first page and told herself that even though she wanted to pour through it as fast as she could, she should read slowly and savor every sentence. Enjoy every character and scene. For the first time since she had been down in this hole, she smiled. Even if there was no one there to see it.

Several hours later, Mari woke from a light sleep. She didn't know if she had been dreaming in her sleep or if it had been almost more of a daydream. In it her brother kept saying, "I'm sorry, Marigold. I'm so sorry." No one had called her by her full given name since she was in grade school. She didn't want to stand out from anyone else because of having a usual name so she demanded everyone call her Mari instead. The dream brought back memories of childhood. Some were okay but most were not what the average person would call good memories. As her mind started wandering to days gone by, she was surprised to hear noise outside. Evan had been here this morning. No one was due back until tomorrow. She felt a chilly fear rise through her. There was no place to hide.

The trap door above her was yanked open and dropped to the floor above with force. Bits of dirt rained down on her.

Mari hadn't realized she was holding her breath until she started feeling light headed.

Evan's voice called down to her with urgency. "Mari, you have to leave. They are coming to get you and I don't know where they will take you. Please, hurry." He threw down a rope.

"Should I try to climb up?" Mari asked without any hesitation. She was more than ready to get out of this nasty place.

"I tied it so you can slip it under your arms. You wouldn't be strong enough to pull yourself up. I'll pull you. I'm sorry. It's probably going to hurt."

She pulled the rope over her head and looped it under her arms. "Ready!" she called up.

Evan pulled and was slightly surprised at how easy it was. Either she was a lot smaller than he had thought or his adrenalin was coursing through him so hard that he had more strength than he believed possible.

Mari reached the top and was dragging herself through the rough opening when she felt her leg being torn by what she imagined was a nail sticking out from the frame around the enclosure. There was no time to worry about that now.

Evan tugged her up to her feet and she had only a second to be embarrassed about what she must have looked like or much less smelled like. He grabbed her arm and started running toward the car waiting outside what she now saw was a large barn in the middle of a field. She couldn't even process that this was the place she had been held captive for so long. She tried to squint at the shock of the bright light but even squinting wasn't allowed by her eyes. They squeezed shut in defiance of the radical change in conditions. She had not seen the light of day for months. Falling to her knees, she quickly jumped back up and let him lead her toward the vehicle.

They had barely left the barn access when she heard the sound of several vehicles roaring up a dirt road. It didn't sound very far away. Pulling her in a different direction from the car, Evan led her around the barn. "Mari," he yelled, "You have to open your eyes. Now!"

She opened them against their will and blinked several times.

"Head in that direction, through that field. Stay low. Go as fast as you can. Don't let them catch you," he said to her in desperation. "I'll delay them as much as possible. Be careful." He let her arm go and ran in the opposite direction.

Mari knew that it must be serious. Had he risked himself to help her? As she stumbled and made her way at what felt like a snail's pace, she wondered how she would know where to go? She looked ahead and saw only fields for as far as her vision would allow. Turning around, she realized that she had no sense of direction. Stopping to catch her breath, she listened carefully to any indication of her surroundings. As she was about to start out again, she heard a gunshot ring out and echo through her mind. Her ears buzzed as if it had been shot right beside her. The next thing she knew, she woke up startled with the realization that someone was carrying her.

Dale slowly opened his eyes against the pounding in his head. It was excruciating and instantly put him in a bad mood. His eyes darted quickly around the small room to take notice of his surroundings. It appeared that he was in a hospital room. Looking towards the door, he noticed a police officer standing at attention in front of the closed exit. It didn't look like the officer was worried about anyone trying to get in but more likely that Dale might try to get out. He acknowledged the monitors that were attached by several cords to several parts of his body. Apparently, it told the hospital staff that he was still alive.

Trying to sit up, the monitors started beeping and within moments, a nurse came into the room. She was followed closely by the officer. The officer took his post at the end of the bed and clasped his hands behind his back. He looked Dale in the face and said in a gruff voice, "Don't try anything, Dale."

Dale just glared at him as the officer kept a careful watch on the situation so the nurse could check his vitals and re-dress his hand. She spoke politely, "I will give you another dose of antibiotics for this infection. It really seems to be helping. The swelling has gone down significantly." She also checked the stitches in his forehead from the whack of the gun. "This is looking better as well. It looks like you will probably be discharged soon."

"Great. What does that mean?" Dale asked with slight sarcasm knowing perfectly well what would happen when he was released from the hospital. Knowing the next destination, he would do whatever he could to stay here as long as possible.

Without moving a muscle, the officer stated with authority, "No worries, Dale. We have a nice place waiting for you. You might even be there in time for lunch."

Not known for his acting abilities, Dale leaned back hard against his pillow and cried out, "My head! The pain! It's unbearable. I need something for it." Feeling gently around the wounded area, he closed his eyes and dramatically stated, "I think it has affected my vision."

Reaching out in front of him, he waved his hand around. "Nurse, are you still here? Nurse?"

The officer couldn't help but smile. He had seen a lot of acting in his days of working hospital watch but this was one of the worst performances he had ever witnessed.

The nurse reassured him, "You've had a CT scan and everything looks just fine. It will be sore for a few days but it's healing nicely."

The officer also gave him some encouragement. "Don't worry, Dale, the prison has a nice medical facility. If you have any trouble, you can always go there for further concerns."

"At least give me something for the pain." Dale snapped. He was starting to feel his anger build. He needed his pills. He didn't like the feeling of being so aware of everything. For him, the dullness was much preferred.

"I just did. It should start working soon," the nurse replied.

Turning from her patient, she started walking toward the door and was surprised when she heard him ask the officer, "Does my wife know I'm here? Someone needs to let her know. She's probably worried about me."

She turned back around and went to the computer to check the chart they had on him. Looking at the officer, they exchanged confused glances.

Dale looked relaxed as he leaned his head back comfortably onto the pillow. "Tell her I'll be coming for her soon."

Chapter 13

Leah looked at the clock, then at her smartwatch, and back to the wall. Feeling heaviness at the weight of time, she tried to distract herself. She wondered if Elinore would sleep the morning through since she had been so adventurous last night. She hoped Daniel would be able to find a safe and comfortable place for her where she would be happy. As much as she already cared for her new friend, she couldn't let her thoughts get distracted.

It had been about 39 hours. The longest 39 hours of her life. Maybe it wouldn't take the full 48. With impatient steps, she walked the house feeling like she was wearing out the floor. She suddenly remembered the pants she had put in the wash yesterday. They most certainly were smelling by now of its day-old washer dampness. She would have to wash them again. Walking into the laundry room, she pulled the mostly dry pants from the wash and shook them out to see if the stain had come out. As she put them back in to wash the freshness back into them, she heard a key in the front door.

With a smile wide enough to hurt her cheeks, she ran across the kitchen just as the door opened. Coming through the doorway was her heart. His smile was as wide as hers as he scooped her into a giant hug.

"You're right on time, Cowboy! Maybe even a touch early," she exclaimed happily.

"Amelia, you did such a good job!" He hugged her until she could hardly breath.

"Did we get him?" She searched his eyes with almost certainty. They had worked so hard for this day.

"We got him. And the big guy. And the information was solid." He looked down into her eyes. "Are you okay? Were you scared?"

"Yes! But I knew you wouldn't let anything happen to me. Did you hear me talking to you?"

"I did. Did you look for me in the shadows?"

"I did. Thank you for sending that car to distract him so I could get away." She looked pleased with herself. "Did they think I was useful?"

"Mrs. Ryan, they thought you did such a good job that you might take over the title of Agent Ryan."

Laughing cheerfully, she put her index finger up to her lips as though thinking seriously. "There is only one Agent Ryan." She playfully tapped her finger on his chest to indicate she was talking about him. "The name Leah has already been used. Plus, Agent Leah isn't very intimidating. Maybe just M. Agent M. You see? Like M-Leah. Amelia."

With a chuckle at her thought process, he said, "That's a stretch."

"We'll work on it. It's not bad. Very James Bond-ish."

"Very." He pulled her into his arms again. "I was so worried about you. It almost drove me mad."

"I have to admit, I was scared."

Looking around the house, he said, "This isn't too bad. Were you comfortable here?"

"It was fine. It's not the same without you. I'm definitely ready to go home."

Pulling her into his arms again, Dallas felt the tension finally drain from deep in his bones. "Me too. Should we pack your stuff up?"

"Sure. It won't take long because I didn't have much with me. Do you want something to eat first?"

"That sounds good." They walked into the kitchen to see what they could whip up to eat. Nodding his head toward the flowers, he questioned, "Those are nice. Where did they come from?"

Smiling sweetly at her husband, she answered with a straight face, "Oh those? Those were brought to me by my neighbor's son when he asked me out on a date."

Looking from the flowers to Amelia's face and back again, he was slow to respond. "I guess I missed that part. No one told me they heard that."

"They were probably afraid of getting punched."
She leaned up on her tiptoes and kissed him on the cheek.

"What else did I miss?" he asked with a tiny bit of aggravation in his voice.

Amelia bit the inside of her lip and squinted her eyes as if in deep concentration. "Let's see." She pretended to think about it for a minute.

Dallas noticed the twitch of her lip in her telltale sign of teasing. "Mrs. Ryan, you are not funny."

Laughing with good humor, she replied, "Really? I think I'm hilarious. Seriously, Mr. Ryan, you know I only have eyes for you. You, my love, are the music to my words."

"And you, my lady, are the words to my music."

Mari was being carried from the field where she had passed out back to the scene at the barn when she started becoming aware of her surroundings. She jerked to awareness just as they were about to set her down on the gurney waiting outside the doors of the ambulance. The

EMT had been flashing his pen light into her eyes when she almost jumped right off the wheeled cot. Her eyes darted around the area in fear.

"It's all right now. The scene has been cleared. We're going to take care of you." The EMT's voice was calming and reassuring.

Mari struggled to sit up. "I heard gun shots. Did anyone get hurt?" She frantically looked around the busy scene loaded with police cars, ambulances, and numerous unmarked vehicles with lights flashing from hidden parts of its exterior. There was so much commotion that it was hard to make sense of anything. Searching each face in the crowd, she started feeling panicked. "Please. Is everyone ok?"

Finally, her eyes locked with a pair of eyes pleading for discovery from the back seat of one of the patrol cars. All noise ceased to be heard. She could only hear the beat of her own heart pounding in her ears. She saw his hand press against the inside of the window. He mouthed the words, "Are you ok?" His expression held concern and compassion.

Before she had a chance to answer, the EMT moved to stand in front of her, blocking her view of Evan. She strained her neck to look around her obstacle but before she could see him again, the patrol car drove off with her only friend in the back seat.

Dallas and Amelia decided to get in a little exercise and enjoy the fresh, crisp air of the early afternoon with a quick walk. They chose to go back to the location where the initial drop off was supposed to take place on the walking trail. Amelia walked him through step by step what had taken place. When she re-told the story about Elinore being so frightened, it made her feel unsettled. Dallas could read her expressions and body language. In an effort to ease her mind, he asked, "Should we stop by and see her after our meeting at headquarters? I would like to meet her."

Smiling at him with appreciation for his concern, she answered, "I would love that."

As they made their way back to the car, another car parked in the lot and a woman with a small boy got out. He ran ahead toward the trail. It looked like he knew where he was going. This obviously wasn't his first time here. Smiling after the child, the woman called out, "Owen, wait for me. You know the rules."

As they walked past each other, the woman and Amelia nodded a greeting to each other and smiled. Understanding how it feels to chase after a child created a bond that felt instant.

Amelia sighed and asked Dallas, "Doesn't it seem like yesterday the kids were that little and we were chasing them all over the place?"

"It sure does." He cocked his head and a twinkle shone in his eye.

She knew that twinkle meant he was about to tease her, so she was ready for it.

"Are you saying you want a baby? Aren't we getting a little old for that?" he questioned.

Stopping in her tracks, she put her hands on her hips and tried to hide her grin. "Well, you might be." Laughing out loud, she grabbed his hand and they continued to the car. "Heavens, no. We're done. I like sleeping through the night too much."

Letting seriousness take over the conversation, he looked at her intensely and asked, "Were you able to sleep through the night when you were worried about the investigation?"

She thought about it for several moments. "I didn't sleep great. But I think I could get used to it. Especially if we didn't have to separate to get the work done."

"I think those assignments are out there. Speaking of, we better head over to the office to get a briefing on the progress of the case. I sure hope it's a lot of good news."

"Me too."

Chapter 14

Mari hadn't slept well even though she had finally been able to rest in the supreme comfort of an actual bed with a pillow-top mattress and high-quality sheets. She had never been one to be able to nap during the day. There were way too many things swirling around in her mind. She had taken several showers in the time since her arrival at the hotel. With hot water nearly burning her, she still hadn't felt like she could ever feel clean again. The struggle with her emotions was overwhelming. She should be elated to be out of her dirt prison. Walking to the window and cracking it open to let in the fresh air, she pondered her future. What would she do now? She had been taken to the hospital to be checked over and received a clean bill of health with the exception of slight malnutrition.

She had been to the police station and had given her statement. She had explained to several people the events that had led up to the day of her rescue. Hoping her detailed accounting of how much hope and help Evan had been to her, she hadn't minded re-telling the hard parts to make sure they knew how he had saved her. Her desperate pleas to be allowed to visit Evan had been granted and she would be going to speak to him tomorrow. Looking around at the elegance of the room, she had never felt more out of place.

Certainly, she didn't have her job any longer. She didn't know for sure but she assumed that she had been evicted from her apartment due to lack of payment for several months. No one could blame the landlords for that. They had no way of knowing her circumstances. Her family, which had recently consisted only of her brother, she now considered non-existent. She would eventually forgive him, but she would never trust him again. Plus, she was sure he would be in jail for a good long while. Her already fractured life had crumbled into ruins and she was left staring down a long, lonely road of uncertainty.

As one tear finally escaped the corner of her eye, she knew the rest would follow. She hadn't allowed herself to cry since being taken from the parking lot a lifetime ago. With one giant tear drop accumulating after another, she didn't know if they would ever stop.

Dallas and Amelia were quietly sitting in the peaceful comfort of each other's company. Dallas reached over to take her hand. He noticed for the first time the bruise on her wrist.

Amelia heard Dallas start breathing heavier and looked up to see fire in his eyes. She looked at his eyes locked onto the black and blue finger outlines of Dales grip. Trying to reassure him, she squeezed his hand as tight as she could and said calmly, "It's fine. It doesn't hurt."

"It's not ok. I don't want you to be in danger like that again. We were right there monitoring the whole thing but something could have gone wrong."

"I knew you wouldn't let anything happen to me. I wasn't worried." She gave him a reassuring smile. "You know what the hardest thing for me was?"

"What?"

"Not wearing my wedding ring." She held up her empty hand. "I felt naked without it."

Reaching into his pocket, he retrieved her ring which he had been carrying with him since she took it off for the mission. "Well, I didn't like it either. Especially now that I know people were trying to make dates with you."

Laughing, she clarified, "It wasn't people. Just one person."

"Just one is one too many." He grinned at her as he took her hand and gently slid her ring back into place.

She held it up in front of her and admired it. "There. That's better."

"Yes." Dallas took her hand and lifted it up to his lips. Kissing her hand, he agreed, "That's better."

Dallas hadn't slept in days. Almost as soon as his head hit the pillow, he was out. Amelia watched him sleep in the dim darkness of early night. She wondered if he would sleep well or if he would wake with the concern of finding where the information they had received would lead. The team had already rescued one victim. There were so many more who needed help.

As Amelia lay in the comfort of her own bed back in her own house, she re-lived the last few days in her mind. The only hiccup had been Elinore and she had been a challenge but she had also been a joy. One quick interaction and she would now be a friend for life. Amelia would see to it that she visited her often. Even though she knew Elinore wouldn't remember her for very long, if at all.

There were some terrifying moments. What if Dale had been able to capture her? That would have put a wrinkle into things. She remembered the vise-like grip he had used on her wrist. Had she been too careless? She thought back carefully to each step from the airport to when Dallas walked through the front door. No. It had all gone according to plan. She had been scared, worried and her pulse had raced into overdrive way too often the last few days. Even though the bruise would subside in color in a few short days, the ordeal might not as quickly release its grip from her memory. But eventually, she knew even that would lose some of its intensity.

Rolling over and placing her hand gently on her husband's chest to feel the rise and fall of his deep sleep breathing, she was glad to get things back to normal. A regular routine. Wasn't that what she thrived on? It was good to know from day to day what was going to happen. No surprises. That's just the way she liked it.

Amelia began thinking about Leah and the way she acted so nervous. It wasn't that much of a stretch. She had listened to everything. Noticed everything. Made sure her address tag was facing just right so Dale couldn't miss it. Remembering his cold, sinister eyes looking right into her at the airport as he was getting arrested made her face the reality of the danger in her choice to be part of the investigation. There was no doubt he had been dangerous. She was thankful to have him off the streets. Unfortunately, there were so many others out there. So many who were arrogantly thinking they would get away with their awful deeds forever. Someone had to find them. Should it be her? Should she continue in this nerve-wracking endeavor?

Listening to her husband's even breathing, Amelia found herself quickly following suit and could feel her body getting heavy with the weight of comfortable sleep. It felt as though she was still only half-dozing when she found herself right back into her dream from the prior night.

She was once again at the vacant airport running out the door and across the tarmac. Up the steps and throwing herself into its lighted opening. Scrambling down the aisle and climbing into the overhead baggage compartment. She could hear the sound of the doors opening one at a time. Shrunk as far back into the tiny area as she could be, she waited in horrifying anticipation as she heard a hand on the latch to her compartment. It popped open and she leaned back expecting to fall again into the dark night and the waiting ground. Instead, once opened, she glimpsed Dallas and his charming grin.

"Why were you hiding? You know you're safe now." His voice was light-hearted and sincere. He reached up and helped her effortlessly down from her fear-filled cubby. Putting his arms around her, he held her tight and spoke words of comfort into her ear.

As she woke from her dream, Amelia felt the familiar weight of security from her husband's arm draped over her. With a deep sigh of contentment, she drifted off into a restful full night of sleep.

Leaving the curtains open to watch the dark expanse of night sky as she lay on the soft-as-silk sheets, Mari thought she might never be comfortable again. She tried desperately to remember the last time she felt honest to goodness comfortable. In her body or in her mind. Beginning to wonder if she was actually a bit crazy, the only place she had felt at home in years is when Evan would sit with his feet dangling over her head talking with her. She initially thought it was because he was her only connection to the outside world. Now that she was in the outside world, she didn't feel like she fit it. Most likely she never had.

What would it be like to see him tomorrow? He would be in jail. Would it be like on tv where he was behind glass and she would have to talk to him through a phone on the wall? Or would it be in a room with a bunch of other people and Evan would be handcuffed to the table? No matter how she thought about it, it was hard to imagine. Maybe he would be mad at her because if he hadn't tried to help her escape, he never would have gotten caught.

The police had sent several people to talk to her. Some talked about what had happened in order to help with the investigation. Some had come in a counseling capacity. She hadn't wanted to talk to any of them but she did cooperate and told them what they wanted to hear.

Mari had watched the sun set earlier. She was surprised to realize how much shorter the days had become since she had last been able to watch the sun at all. Shorter daylight hours actually made her feel like the days were longer. She found herself contemplating the reality that when the days had longer daylight hours, she couldn't wait for the cozy feeling of shorter days. During shorter days, she was anxiously awaiting the longer days. When was the last time she was actually content right where she was? Once it was acknowledged, would she even be able to make the conscious decision to appreciate her current state? With the heaviness of her thoughts, she found it hard to believe that there would come a day when she would simply value each moment as it was intended.

Staring up at the dark, star-filled sky, she wondered if she should have had someone look at her leg. They had cleaned the wound from the rusty nail and had wrapped it at the hospital. They had even given her a tetanus shot since she wasn't aware of ever getting one before. The nail had really dug into her skin. Right now, it was burning as a reminder of Evan saving her from her dark hole. At the moment, she felt like she was in a different kind of dark hole. Was there any way to escape this one?

As she drifted off into a restless sleep, she quickly started dreaming. *Mari was back in the confines of her dirt prison. There was dim light. Just enough to see the gecko scurry up to her. She reached over and lifted it into her hand. "Hello, my friend. Where have you been?" Her voice sounded strange to her own ears. She never had reason to speak aloud unless Evan was visiting.*

Hearing some movement overhead, she was anticipating with happiness the door opening to reveal Evan. Instead, the door opened and dropped to the ground sending little cascades of dirt down onto the floor around her. Her brother stood at the opening along with another man who she didn't recognize but was instantly wary of. He had a coldness to his stare that made her feel chilled to the bone.

The gecko ran from her hand and up the wall continuing up her brother's pants leg and ending up sitting on his shoulder. Her brother looked down at Mari with contempt on his face. Looking into the face of the brother who she used to swing high enough to reach the sky, she couldn't help but ask, "Why did you let this happen?"

With a sneer and callousness in his voice, he looked at the small critter on his shoulder and said, "You thought he was your friend. He's with me." Turning on his heel, her brother walked away.

Feeling the sting of his words, she held back her tears as she looked fearfully into the face of the man who still glared down at her. "Why are you doing this?" Mari called up from the dark floor.

Reaching behind him, the man yanked Evan over to the opening so she could see him. With shock in her eyes, she didn't understand what was happening. With a *voice like she imagined the devil would have, he stared into her eyes as he said, "You thought he was your friend." She looked over to Evan and saw the man holding him twitch as he pulled a gun from inside his jacket and shot Evan in the head. Evan fell forward and landed at her feet.*

Mari woke up soaked in sweat and screaming. Taking in her surroundings, she quickly quit by putting a hand over her mouth. Her body shook with sobs for several minutes. Was this the beginning of a different kind of nightmare? She would have preferred the solitude of her dark hole to this. She lay in the big, comfortable bed feeling more confined than she had in months. Staring out the window, she watched the sky change from the dark of night to the dusk of early morning. She didn't want to close her eyes for fear of what might come in her sleep.

Chapter 15

Amelia woke feeling energized after a refreshing night of deep sleep. She felt ready to take on all the challenges the day would hold. She and Dallas started the day with a cup of steaming coffee and banana bread which the chief's wife had dropped off on the front step the day before. Over a lively conversation about the upcoming day's events, it was agreed that an update on the status of the kidnapped prisoners was what they were the most interested in. They were due for the briefing at 9:00 and until then, they would relax and just enjoy each other's company.

Amelia kept thinking about things she forgot to tell Dallas. She told him how she didn't dare look for him at the airport for fear of happy recognition showing in her emotions and blowing their cover. She knew he had overheard what took place within the house but she enjoyed telling him about meeting the nosey neighbor while going for a walk with Elinore and the fear she felt while driving to the used car parking lot to meet Dale just to name a few. He listened with interest and didn't have much to share with her since all of his time had been spent at the station stuck in an office worried about her.

Mari woke with a pounding headache and slight nausea. She assumed it was from the drastic change in her daily routine. She had left the curtains open and even though the sun had poured through into the room, she had slept longer than she expected. Climbing out of the unnecessarily large bed, she wondered what the day would hold. How long would she be able to stay here? She knew she had to devise a plan to move on with her life, but frankly, she didn't even know where to begin. As her feet hit the floor, pain shot up through her leg. Looking down at the source of the pain, she realized the bandage had come off during the night and she saw a substance oozing out of the wound. The doctor had said if it didn't start looking better in a day or two, to come back in to have it checked again. Realizing that if she would have just agreed to take the antibiotics as originally instructed, she probably wouldn't be in this predicament. However, now she didn't know what she would be expected to pay for and she certainly didn't have money for doctors or medicine.

She would think about it later. Right now, she had to get showered and ready to see Evan. She had been thinking about him non-stop and she wondered if she had crossed his mind as well. He had never seen her cleaned up, but as she stood in front of the mirror, she was disappointed at what she saw. Looking back at her was someone she hardly recognized. Someone who was pale and gaunt, with sunken eyes and unkept, overgrown hair. She thought the reflection looked old and extremely worn out.

Well, there wasn't much to do about any of those things, at least not at the moment. Thinking a hot shower

221

might lift her spirits, she put a pod of coffee in the maker and hit start before heading toward the hope of washing the dread off herself.

Dale was more than happy to cooperate with the investigation as long as he felt in control of his eventual release. After all, they didn't have anything on him directly. He was the ultimate victim. They hadn't found anything incriminating against him. He was just in the wrong place at the wrong time. He didn't even need a lawyer to explain that. He would hold on to his knowledge about Big Fish in case he needed it down the road. He almost laughed at learning that Big Fish's name was actually Wade. That didn't seem very intimidating at all.

After being released from the hospital yesterday, he had been transported to a prison cell presumable in the same town since the drive hadn't been very long.

The guard came to get him with the announcement that he had a visitor. Being shuffled into an interrogation room, he started making his demands. "I will need a cup of steaming hot coffee with four packs of regular sugar, no cream. Also, maybe a few cookies or some kind of chips. I'm not really picky about my snacks." He leaned back in his chair and crossed his ankles while intertwining his fingers in his lap. He felt relaxed and was looking forward to a visit. Although his head was achy, he was feeling even more alert as time went past without those unnecessary pills. Looking back, he wondered if things would have gone differently if he had forgone the pills which he now realized were meant to be a distraction implemented by Wade.

The door opened and a rather large man appeared in the doorway. He walked over to the table and pulled out the chair with his foot. He sat military straight, crossing his arms over his chest, staring at Dale with a look of authority. Dale wasn't intimidated. He stared back with contempt.

"My name is Agent Ryan. I have been assigned to your case for quite some time. You gave us a bit of a run for a while, but you got sloppy."

Dale felt his posture change from relaxed to annoyed. With a puff of disgust, he replied, "I didn't get sloppy. You've got nothing on me."

Agent Ryan nodded his head. "Oh, but you did. Plus, we got your Big Fish talking up a storm. He gave up the information with hardly any fight. He threw you under the bus so fast it was almost too easy."

Dale didn't know if this was a test or if the investigator was being serious. He could see Big Fish turning on him. Anything to save his own pathetic self.

"We got the names, places, dates. We don't need you for anything. You and your buddy Wade and all the others are finally getting what's coming to you."

Knowing it was true since the Agent surely had the information from the suitcase, he conceded. "I worked my butt off for these people. I was just a link in their chain. This was the end of the line. I was about to get a decent pay out, take my wife and start a new life together in a new place. I was finally going to get what I deserved."

Agent Ryan stood up and towered over Dale. He leaned over, placing his hands flat on the table and stared a hole into Dale's eyes. "She is MY wife, and oh, trust me, you are definitely going to get what you deserve."

As Dallas was in with Dale, Amelia was in a conference room waiting for him to finish so they could go together into the briefing. She was surprised it was taking so long since she didn't think Dale would be cooperative enough to talk. As Amelia read through the files about the young women who had been held captive, one in particular grabbed her attention. Her name was Marigold; she was a local girl and her story broke Amelia's heart. Marigold's landlord reported her missing after not receiving rent for two months in a row. During the missing person investigation, it was discovered that her boss hadn't missed her. He had just assumed she moved on to something else. No family reported her missing. It appeared that she didn't have any friends or anyone who cared at all about her. Her brother was in custody for his involvement in the whole ordeal and he had never tried to rescue her or tried to help her in any way. It was unimaginable to Amelia that someone could slip through the cracks so easily.

As she came to the end of the file, her interest perked up a bit at the involvement of one of the kidnappers. A young man by the name of Evan had put up quite a fight to ensure that the police search and find Marigold in the corn fields. According to the report by the arresting officer, Evan fought like a dog for them to find her and would not cooperate until he saw her being carried out of the field and taken into the ambulance. Since then, he had been agreeable and answered any questions thrown at him.

Amelia was about to read through Evan's file when the door opened and her husband stood in the doorway with a handful of papers and a grin. "Are you ready for your first official run-down?"

She stood up with nervous excitement and held up the file on Marigold. "Can I take this with me for a while?"

With a nod and a quick glance at the label, he gave consent with a reminder that it couldn't leave the building.

They walked close enough to feel the heat from each other's arms which gave Amelia an added boost of confidence. As they were nearing the briefing room, a thin, tiny young woman walked toward them looking at the room numbers on the doors. Her eyes were dark-circled and scared. Amelia instantly recognized her from the photo in the file she still held in her hand. She felt a fierce protectiveness come over her. She stopped in her tracks as her breath caught in her throat. Dallas noticed her delay and stopped to look back at her. He eyed the fragile girl who had drawn his wife's attention. Amelia reached out her hand to catch the attention of her interest.

With frightened eyes, the girl stopped and looked down at Amelia's feet. Amelia slowly reached her hand out to touch Marigold's hand but it was pulled away and clasped together with her other hand. Her hands held on to each other with knuckle white grip in front of her body.

Amelia fought the urge to let tears fall. Quietly, she spoke to her. "Marigold?"

Dallas took note of the interaction and continued his way down the hall. He would meet up with his wife in the briefing room.

A voice so quiet it could hardly be heard answered, "Yes." Still not making eye contact, she looked at the hand reaching out to her.

Amelia turned her hand over and held her palm up, reaching a few inches closer to Marigold's clasped hands. Just above a whisper, Amelia spoke to the broken young woman, "Marigold, I see you. I hurt for you. I am here for you. I am your friend. Please let me help you." They stood quietly next to each other for several minutes. Amelia couldn't hear any noise coming from Marigold but as she continued to watch her bowed head, she noticed large tear drops falling off her cheeks and traveling a long, straight path to splash into evaporation on the ground by her feet. Amelia moved her outstretched hand a few inches closer and with joy and sorrow, she witnessed Marigold's hands release their tight grip and with hesitation, slowly reach over and place her small, pale hand delicately on top of Amelia's. Gently closing it in a warm, tender squeeze, she reassured her with the vow, "You're going to be ok. I promise."

With a shaky intake of breath, Marigold looked up into Amelia's eyes and felt certain that she heard the truth. Relief and a hundred other mixed emotions all released at the same time and she fell into Amelia's waiting arms. Her tears were gone and she felt overwhelmed with hope and optimism. After standing in the middle of the hallway for several minutes with people occasionally passing by. Amelia led Marigold over to some chairs lined up against the wall. They sat for the time it took for Amelia to explain who she was and why she was there. Marigold explained that she was there to talk to Evan. They agreed to meet back at the same chairs when they were done with their respective conversations. "We'll work it out, Marigold. You have my word."

Marigold looked into Amelia's eyes with a worried, furrowed brow. "Amelia. Could I ask you a favor? I know we just met and I don't normally ask for favors, but it's important to me."

With a reassuring smile, Amelia replied, "I can't promise anything but whatever it is, I can promise I will try my best. What can I do?"

Feeling her mouth go dry, she licked her lips and bit her bottom lip before slowly nodding her head and looking right into Amelia's eyes. "Can you try to help Evan too? I know he did wrong but he's not a bad person. He was just with bad people. It wasn't his fault." Marigold held her breath as she waited for the answer.

Reaching over to take her hand again, Amelia squeezed it and promised, "I believe that to be true. Yes. I will listen to his story and do my best to see that the truth comes out and justice will be upheld on every level of this field."

With a big release of air and a fresh brightness to her eyes, she thanked her new ally.

"I'll see you back here in just a little bit. Good luck." Amelia gave Marigold a big, encouraging smile.

They both went in different directions with similar feelings of uplifted spirits and hope overflowing.

232

Chapter 16

The briefing went as well as could be expected. Everyone had high praise for Amelia's performance. There was a lot of information passed around about others involved along with additional victims. They were continuing to locate and rescue the kidnapped. Dale and Wade both broke under interrogation and were still letting information slip on a regular basis. Dale was trying to convince the jailer that his pain was so severe that he must be taken immediately back to the hospital or at least given some good drugs. His days of manipulation were gone and he had lost his edge with one too many bad choices.

Amelia had discussed several options and opportunities that she thought would be helpful for Marigold and some inquiries were already being made. She laid out her case in support of leniency on Evan after inquiring more into his background. It appeared as if he was just a pawn in the grand scheme of things.

The room Mari had been taken to was small and well-lit with a table in the middle and a chair on each side of the table. The only other thing in the room was a large mirror that she was certain was actually a window and she felt uncomfortable knowing she was being watched.

She sat rigid in her chair waiting for the door across from her to open. She jumped as the door behind her opened and someone came in carrying two glasses of water. "Would you care for a drink?" they asked pleasantly. "I could get you some juice or soda if you prefer." They set the two glasses at the appropriate places on the table.

"Thank you. Water is fine."

Finding herself alone again in the room, she started nervously biting her thumb nail. It was a terrible habit she did only when she was nervous. Obviously, she had chewed off her nails over the last months but she couldn't help herself. Pulling her hand away, she reached down and maneuvered her sitting position to include sitting on her hands so she wouldn't keep biting. She was looking at the scarred markings on the table and giving a story to some of them in her mind when the door opened slowly.

Evan stood in the doorway with his hands and feet in cuffs. She could feel her heartbeat in her throat.

The guard nudged him slightly so he moved into the room. He went to the table and sat down, never taking his eyes off of her. After taking his seat, the guard attached his cuffs to a place on the edge of the table and on the floor. He turned and left the room, closing the door behind him.

They were alone in the room but both knew they were not alone in their conversation.

Evan's eyes scanned Mari's face. He could barely speak. "Are you okay?" he choked out the whispered question.

"Yeah. I saw them take you in the police car. Are you okay? I heard a gunshot. I didn't know." She swallowed. "I didn't know. Did you…" She couldn't come up with words.

"I'm okay. It was all kind of a blur. I'm so sorry I didn't get there sooner. I was so worried about you. No one would tell me anything about you. I saw them carry you out of the fields and," his voice cracked and he looked down at the table.

Mari took over the conversation in order to give him a minute to compose himself. "They got my brother. And yours."

Evan raised his eyebrows in surprise. "Really?" His eyes clouded over. "Good riddance. I hope I never see him again."

"Agreed."

With a look of concern, he asked, "Are you safe?"

With a shrug, Mari answered, "I think so.

Motioning his hand around the room indicating the whole area, his cuffs clinked noisily. "If I ever get out of here, I will keep you safe. You can be sure of that." With a warm heat filling his face, he added quietly, "That is, if you would want me to."

With a fear of uncertainty, she replied with caution. "One step at a time. You have to get out first."

Happy that it wasn't a flat-out rejection, Evan grinned. It was followed quickly by a serious tone. He gazed at her with a look she didn't recognize. She wasn't used to caring affection. "Mari." He reached toward her but the clinking of his handcuffs wouldn't allow him to reach far. "I won't let you down."

The door opened and the guard entered the room. Evan kept his eyes locked onto Mari's as his cuffs were unlocked and he was led toward the exit. As he left the room, he felt encouraged at his belief that he just witnessed the slight curve indicating the start of a smile touching the corners of Mari's lips. What he wouldn't give to see a genuine smile on her face. He would do everything in his power to make it happen.

Chapter 17

One Week Later

It had been a long week. Daily meetings for updates along with continued work to guarantee there was no doubt about the convictions for the guilty parties. While Amelia had chosen not to have any contact with Dale, Dallas met with him several times. Each time revealed a little more information about how long this twisted scheme had been going on. With Dale being off the drugs which had been freely given to him by Wade, he was more alert and there was no more talk of his imaginary wife.

It was too late to help some of the victims, but they were able to locate and save dozens of individuals who had given up on ever receiving the help they needed. Amelia had met with several young women in the area who had been affected by the traumatizing events. They had even reunited some families with loved ones they thought were lost to them forever.

Amelia had made such a strong connection with Marigold that she felt almost like she was her own child. Each day she could see some improvement in Marigold. Not just in her physical health and appearance but also in her state of mind.

The sun had brought some color back to Mari's face. She looked stronger and wasn't as jittery as she had been. Amelia was going to meet Mari for lunch during her break at work. With much anticipation, Amelia walked into the brightly lit building and signed it at the front desk. Making her way through the quiet, carpeted corridor of Graceful Peace Nursing Home, she found herself humming along with the relaxing music floating in the air. She could hear the sounds of dishes clanking and the smells of what was sure to be a delicious lunch. Before getting to the dining room, she veered right and made her way to Elinore's room.

Elinore sat in the wingback chair facing the window. She was staring out at the bird sitting on the feeder. Amelia had visited every day and each one was different. She didn't know what to expect today. Knocking softly on the open door before entering, she cheerfully called out, "Hello, Elinore! It's your friend Leah." She walked over to Elinore's chair and squatted down to her eye level.

Elinore looked at her for several seconds before smiling at her. "Hello, dear. Where have you been? I haven't seen you in ages."

Not wanting to remind her of her visit the day prior, she just smiled back, "I've missed you. I came to see if you want to have lunch with me and a friend."

"What's for lunch?" Elinore asked as she lifted her nose into the air to see if the aroma smelled appealing.

"I'm not sure, but I'm sure we can arrange for something you would like."

"Ok. Will the kids be coming? I guess probably not. They should be taking lunch at school."

"No. Not the kids. But my friend Marigold will be joining us." Just as Amelia finished the statement, Mari walked into the room.

With a look of concern on her face, she asked hesitantly, "Am I interrupting you? I can wait outside."

Before Amelia could respond, Elinore spoke with joy in her voice, "Goldie! Come in. Come in. Look at you so beautiful today!"

Mari's face turned red and she looked at her feet. "Hello, Miss Elinore." She crossed the room and took the extended hand that was reaching out for her.

Elinore grasped Mari's hand and brought it to her cheek. She looked over at Amelia. "Goldie has been here taking such good care of me. She is simply pure gold."

Amelia felt her heart skip a beat at the look that passed between the two individuals who had nothing but so much in common. Their instant bond was plain to see.

"Thank you, Miss Elinore." Using her free hand to swipe at a tear about to leave the corner of her eye, she glanced over at Amelia's beaming face.

Amelia leaned forward and embraced Mari in a quick hug. "I'm so glad you could get time from work to join us for lunch. Is your day going well?"

Mari nodded and with the slightest hint of a smile, she replied, "Yes. I feel bad calling it work. It's so much fun."

"You are already spoken of very highly. I feel like royalty every time I come in these days because everyone is so thankful for me referring you."

With another blush at the second compliment, Mari looked back toward Elinore. "Are you ready for lunch? I made sure the tea is just how you like it." She helped Elinore up from the chair.

"Thank you, dear. Let's go see what they are offering for lunch. I'm not picky since I don't have to cook it myself. It's bound to be good." With plenty of energy, she put her arms through Mari's and Amelia's to make their way to the dining room. With linked arms, they looked like childhood friends as they made an entrance into the large gathering of those already seated for their meal. Several other residents of the nursing home offered pleasant greetings to Elinore and Mari. Mari knew all of them by name and she responded like she had been here for years instead of mere days.

It had been a pleasant meal with lively conversation between Elinore and Amelia. Mari was quiet but would join in occasionally. As the staff came around with a cart loaded up with various desserts to choose from, Elinore looked across the room and her hand raised in a wave. Daniel smiled and made his way across the dining room spreading hellos along the way. Reaching the table, he leaned down to kiss his mother's cheek before taking the fourth chair at the table.

Elinore exclaimed with a teasing tone, "Did you know it was just now time for dessert?"

With a chuckle, he replied, "Of course. And since I already ate lunch, I'm all set for it." He pointed at the coconut cream pie. "That piece has my name of it." He greeted Mari and Amelia. "I'm not interrupting a girl's lunch, am I?"

Mari quickly shook her head and looked down at the table.

Amelia grinned and replied, "You're right on time. We just finished talking about you."

With a grimace, Daniel moaned, "I can imagine!"

After some small talk and a taste of dessert, everyone leaned back feeling relaxed. Elinore looked across the table at Amelia. She smiled but it didn't quite reach her eyes like usual. "Are you here visiting someone, dear?"

Without missing a step, Amelia answered, "I am. I came to have lunch with two very special friends to whom I have recently become acquainted."

"That's nice." She looked at Mari and noticed her name tag. "Do you work here Mari?"

"Yes, ma'am, I do." Mari reached over to touch Elinore's hand which was lying on the table. "Are you ready to go back to your room?"

Elinore looked around at unfamiliar faces in an unfamiliar place. "My room?"

Mari got up from her seat and reached out her hand to Elinore. "I still have a few minutes before I have to start back so we could walk outside for a few breaths of fresh air."

"Well, that would be lovely. You're a sweet girl." Reaching for Mari's hand, she allowed herself to be lead from the room.

Daniel and Amelia got up to follow behind. As they were walking through the double doors leading to the park-like courtyard, Amelia heard a familiar voice coming up behind her.

"Hello all!"

Everyone turned to the pleasant greeting. With a large grin, Amelia took several strides over to kiss her husband. "Hey Cowboy! This is a nice surprise. If you had been five minutes earlier, you could have joined us for dessert."

"That's okay. I'll have extra with supper tonight."
Dallas nodded a greeting to Mari. "Good to see you,
Marigold. Is everything going well for you?"

Nodding her head and looking past him instead of
at him, she replied a quiet, "Yes, sir. Thank you."

"Elinore, you look lovely today." Dallas directed
the compliment to a smiling face.

With a devilish look bordering on flirtation, she
replied, "Thank you. You are a handsome fellow, aren't
you?" Her gaze slid to Amelia. "Is he with you?"

Putting her arm through the crook of Dallas', she
answered, "He is. Aren't I the lucky one?"

With slight hesitation, Daniel reached out his
hand. "You're Leah's husband?"

With a hearty hand shake, Dallas replied, "I am."

Clearing his throat several times, Daniel nodded
as he said, "I'm sorry I asked your wife out on a date."

With a chuckle, Dallas said good naturedly,
"Apology accepted. Who could blame you?" He looked at
his wife and winked.

Elinore and Mari looked at him with surprise registering in their expressions.

Not wanting to embarrass Daniel, Amelia bit her tongue to keep from laughing out loud. The looks on her friend's faces were priceless. She held up her hand to get everyone's attention. "It was just a misunderstanding."

Everyone just made noises in their throats that sounded like confused acceptance. Not able to help herself, she had to add, "But the flowers were beautiful."

Looking to her friends' confusion, she said, "I'll tell you about it one of these days."

Before too many questions were raised, Dallas said, "Marigold, would you be able to come to our house for dinner tonight? I have something to discuss with you."

Amelia looked at Dallas' face with eyebrows raised. He nodded his answer to the unasked question. Her smile couldn't be hidden. "I can pick you up at the end of your shift," she said.

Mari looked a little scared. "Okay."

With reassurance, Dallas said, "It's all good stuff. Nothing to worry about."

"Okay." She didn't know these people very well yet, but she already felt that she could trust them. And she didn't trust anyone. "Miss Elinore, are you ready to go to your room?"

"Yes, dear." She looked at the other three people standing next to her and smiled. With a smile and what looked almost like a curtsy, she said, "It was nice meeting you all."

As Mari led her toward the door to go back inside, Daniel's face fell.

With sadness in his voice, Daniel said, "It's a good thing we found such a nice place for her. She's safe here."

Amelia responded, "Yes. And she is loved. She knows that."

Amelia was just driving into the parking lot when she saw Marigold leave the front door of the nursing home. Glancing in both directions with uncertainty radiating from her demeanor, Mari relaxed slightly at the sight of Amelia's vehicle driving up. As she looked back at the building which had become a temporary safe haven for her, Mari could see several faces watching her from the room windows facing the parking lot. With a nod and a wave in their direction, she acknowledged her audience. Some of them most likely didn't even know who she was and others didn't see anything past their stares of blindness. Several just enjoyed watching the comings and goings of the building while a few only wanted to feel the warmth from the end of the day sunshine. No matter which situation they were in, Mari was delighted to be a part of each one's life. She would prosper here. She had never felt more at home anywhere.

As she climbed into the passenger seat of the car, she acknowledged the pleasant greeting addressed to her with one of her own. She was getting more comfortable with Amelia and wouldn't allow herself to be afraid to get attached. Everyone else in her life had let her down, but she felt optimistic that she might have found someone who would actually care about what happened to her. It was a very unusual but hopeful feeling.

Amelia instantly started chatting. "How was your afternoon?"

"It was good. It seemed to fly by."

"How is the cut on your leg? Do you think it needs one more look at it?"

"No. It's much better. It's probably going to leave a scar but that's okay. It's getting better every day."

"Sometimes a scar can be a visual reminder of something incredible that has been overcome. I'm so sorry that happened to you. But I'm thankful that you made it out of there. Look at how many peoples' lives you are brightening every day just by being you. It's amazing. I watched you interact with the residents today and you seemed completely at ease with it. Like you have known them and have been working there for years. It's quite something."

Looking over at Amelia's profile instead of at her hands in her lap for a change, she answered not quite as

251

timidly to the compliment as before, "Thank you. I love it. I feel like I belong there. Maybe I can actually make a difference."

"Of course you can. You are already. It's extraordinary to see the result of just a few pleasant words or the slightest acknowledgment of a person. Just a simple hand shake, hug or pat on the arm. Everyone craves some form of contact. Too many people who end up in nursing homes are just left to themselves and ignored or brushed aside. Your kindness to them will be priceless." Amelia glanced over to see Marigold nodding her agreement.

Biting the inside of her bottom lip, Mari was afraid to ask the question. But her curiosity got the better of her. "Can I ask what's happening tonight? I mean, I'm thankful for the invitation for supper but, there isn't bad news with it, is there?"

Reaching across the car's console to pat Mari's arm, she replied, "No. Nothing bad. We have learned a lot of new information about the investigation today and we thought you would like to be updated too."

With surprise arching her eyebrows, she answered, "Of course. Thank you. I didn't think I would be kept informed or ever know the outcome of anything."

"Well, you should know all of the updates because you were a big part of what happened and it affected your life in a huge way." Seeing the calm reaction to the news, Amelia had something else to add which she didn't know if it would be received the same way. "So, that being said, I want to ask you something."

Mari turned slightly in her seat to give Amelia her full attention. "Okay."

Smiling at her trust and respect, Amelia gave her some unexpected information. "Well, as you know, this will be a long process and we are doing everything in our power to see it through as quickly as possible. Dallas did a little negotiating and worked some magic. How would you feel about Evan joining us for dinner tonight also? He would be under Dallas' supervision; he would be wearing an ankle monitor and it will only be for a few hours before he has to return to the jail."

Mari was speechless. Was it possible to have a hundred thoughts flying through your mind at one time? The thought of seeing Evan again almost took her breath away. All she could do was nod her head.

Cheerfully, Amelia started chatting again. "Let's stop at your room at the hotel so you can freshen up if you want. I made a lasagna for supper. Do you like lasagna?" To the nod of affirmation, she continued, "We'll have a salad and bread with it. What about dessert? We just have ice cream. Is there anything special that sounds good to you? We can stop and get something on the way."

Feeling her throat get tight with emotion, Mari marveled at the conversation. No one had ever asked her what she wanted to eat. Shaking her head she was about to give a reply of "no" when something crossed her mind. "Would we be able to stop somewhere and get some Junior Mints? Evan mentioned that they were his favorite candy of all time. That would be considered dessert, wouldn't it?"

Laughing at the animation in Mari's voice, Amelia was quick to respond, "I think that can be arranged!"

Evan was surprised when Agent Ryan came to his cell door and opened it up. "Are you up for a change of scenery?"

Without hesitating, Evan didn't question him. He just jumped up from his thin mattress and followed.

Dallas handed him a bag that had the clothes he had been wearing the day he was arrested. He knew Evan would want to get out of the prison scrubs. The clothes had been released from evidence and Dallas had taken them home to be washed in preparation for this dinner. It had been fun planning this evening with his wife. She had been so enthusiastic that he couldn't help joining in.

Leaving the jail, Dallas filled him in on the evening's plans. "I got you out for a few hours. We have to report back here by 8:00. How would you feel about supper with Amelia and me tonight? Lasagna."

"That sounds great! Thank you." Evan's voice was filled with gratitude.

Stopping on the sidewalk to pay attention to his response, Dallas asked, "How about if Marigold joins us?"

Pulling his head back as if slapped, his eyes got the slightest bit rounder. "No." He reached up and rubbed his hand over his mouth. He looked at Dallas with fear of disappointment lurking in the depths of his eyes. "Are you serious?"

Dallas grinned at the look of complete shock. "Yes. I'm serious."

Evan crossed his arms in front of himself and looked from the ground to the sky to Dallas to the sky again. "You're serious?"

"Yes."

Looking down at his prison attire, he looked back with questions waiting to be asked. "Does she know I will be there?"

"Yes."

"And she's okay with that?"

"Yes."

A look of hope filled his face. "Wow. This is unexpected."

"Well, let's get going. You can clean up at the house." They happened to be walking by a flower shop located in between the jail and the funeral home. Evan glanced in the window. Dallas stopped at the door and pulled out his wallet. "I'll spot you." He handed Evan several bills and followed him inside. He hated having to be right with Evan as if he didn't trust him, but it was part of the agreement he had made with the station to allow his release for the evening.

Evan walked right up the counter and asked the clerk, "Do you have any Marigolds?"

"I do. Would you like them in an arrangement or by themselves?" the woman asked politely.

"They are perfect all by themselves. Thank you." Evan watched the woman pick out a nice array of varying shades of yellow, orange and even some red. As they left the florist's shop, Evan handed Dallas all of the change he received from the transaction. "I owe you $23.95. It will be the first payment I make as soon as I have employment."

"I don't doubt that." Dallas said with encouragement.

When they arrived at the house, Dallas showed Evan to the guest bathroom where there were supplies laying out for a shave and a clean-up. "Feel free to take a shower or whatever you like. The ladies will be here in about 30 minutes."

Reaching out and firmly shaking Dallas' hand, Evan said, "I don't know what I did to deserve your help, but I do really appreciate it."

"I know you do. You're a good kid with a promising future. You just have to stay on the right track, and something tells me that you will." Dallas smacked him on the shoulder and turned to walk to the kitchen.

Chapter 18

As Amelia and Marigold walked into the house, the delicious smells drifting from the kitchen made it feel comfortable and inviting. Marigold was wringing her hands with nervous anticipation. She didn't know what it would be like to see Evan for the first time in such a setting. Amelia had helped her with her hair and she had applied just a touch of makeup. She picked out a simple cotton summer dress from the bag of clothes she had received earlier in the week from a women's organization.

They entered the kitchen and Dallas was standing by the oven, peeking in to check on the lasagna. "Hey! You're right on time." He observed the nervous-looking girl. "How are you, Marigold?"

"Fine. Thank you." She surveyed her surroundings and sadness crossed her whole body. Her shoulders slumped, her forehead creased, her mouth turned downward, her head hung. "Evan decided not to come?" she asked quietly.

"I wouldn't have missed it for the world." Evan's voice sounded deeper than she had memorized in her mind.

Her head popped up to see him standing in the hallway holding a handful of Marigolds and looking at her with eyes of cautious expectation.

Amelia walked over to take an exaggerated long look at the progress of the oven's contents with Dallas. With their backs turned, Evan and Mari had as much privacy as they would be allowed at this point.

Not completely knowing what the other was feeling, neither knew how to act. Evan held out the flowers and smiled slightly. Marigold looked at the simple yet beautiful gesture and then looked right into Evan's eyes. Once her smile started, she couldn't contain it. It spread across her face until it reached so far it caused a small wrinkle in the corner of each eye. Evan had craved that smile. It made his breath catch.

He took the first step from the hallway into the kitchen. She met him partway. As they wrapped each other in an embrace that felt like home, both were aware that they were fortunate to be standing there together. So many things could have happened or gotten in the way. Wanting to stay there in each other's arms indefinitely, they knew it was crucial to be appropriate and take things slowly. Separating seemed impossible but necessary. Surprisingly, Mari was the first to speak. "Can I help you set the table?"

Amelia cheerfully accepted the invitation. Everyone pitched in to help and they were all seated at the table enjoying their meal in no time. While Dallas and Amelia did most of the small talk, the others occasionally piped up for the discussion. Marigold and Evan hardly broke eye contact the entire time. Dallas leaned back in his chair and said, "I'm stuffed. I always eat just a little too much when it comes to pasta."

"Me too." Amelia agreed.

Mari got up from the table and went to retrieve her purse. Pulling from it a theater sized box of Junior Mints, she poured them into the empty bowl she had placed on the counter earlier while setting the table. Glancing shyly over to see Evan's reaction, she was surprised to see a look resembling pain instead of happiness on his face.

She tilted her head in confusion. He looked at her and with amazement he asked, "You were stuck down there with nothing and you remembered a conversation about my favorite candy?"

She looked at him with appreciation. "I wasn't there with nothing. I had a penlight, a book, and memories of our conversations. It got me through."

They sat in silence, each remembering their own thoughts of their time together.

Dallas broke through after several minutes to announce, "Let's leave these dishes until later and settle in the living room. We have a couple updates to share."

Evan reached into the bowl of mints and grabbed a few to pop into his mouth as they got up from the table.

Taking seats in the comfortable living room, Evan and Marigold seemed to be on edge now that the tone of the conversation was more serious.

Dallas tried to break the ice with a light-hearted comment, "Relax, it's not bad news. You both look like you are headed to the firing squad."

With the smallest of grins, Evan and Marigold seemed to lean back a little more in their chairs. They both trusted these new people in their lives. A unique experience for each.

Dallas glanced at Amelia and she gave him a nod indicating that he should be the one to start the conversation.

"Ok. So, I won't bore you with the details but as you know, we have both of your brothers in custody. They have been indicted and charged and will be sentenced in the near future. We also made it several rungs up the ladder and have done the same with those individuals. We have complete confidence that with the detailed information we have, there is no question of lots of prison time for each. That being said, while we caught the so-called "Big Fish" and even many others in his group, along with several even bigger fish, we are still working on catching the "Whale". Our nets are spread wide and we'll get him eventually. In the meantime, we feel that you will be safe. You two were just minnows or bait you could say. Caught up in the middle."

Amelia couldn't help but laugh. "That's a lot of fishing references."

Dallas chuckled, "I agree. But the water holds secrets. Dangers lurk under its depts that we would never imagine. But we have your backs. You can come to us with any concerns or questions along the way."

Evan couldn't help adding, "So, you could say you are our lifeboat?" He grinned, lightening the mood.

"Yes, you could say that." Dallas replied with a chuckle and a feeling of assurance that everyone was on the same page.

"Ok." Dallas continued while turning his attention more to Evan, "Evan, I have a friend who owns a construction business in town. He could use an extra pair of hands. I have talked to the attorney and the judge and they both agree that the situation seems appropriate to allow you to do work release. This means that you will be allowed to leave each day to report to work and only work and then return to lockup as soon as you are done with work. If you prove yourself, and I know you will, you can stay on after your sentence is completed." He waited for a response.

"I appreciate the opportunity and the confidence. I won't let you down. Thank you." Evan stood up and reached over to shake Dallas' hand. Ideas were already starting to formulate in his mind. "I will save every penny so when I'm released, I will be able to start fresh." He looked at Mari and his expression reminded her of a child getting a puppy for Christmas. She was so happy for him.

Amelia continued the conversation. "Marigold, I have spoken with the nursing home. They loved you from the first moment they met you. You have been such a blessing to them. It's hard to find someone so caring and devoted. They informed me that they have several rooms at the end of the East wing that are used as short-term accommodations for visiting family members or staffing emergencies. They want me to let you know that they are offering you one of those rooms so you can leave the hotel and have more of place of your own. You won't be committed to any more work or hours if you accept it. It is yours for as long as you want it."

Tears were flowing from Marigold's eyes. Evan reached across the coffee table for a tissue and sat close to her on the couch while wiping her tears. She took the damp cloth and leaned into him.

"Mari, that's amazing!" Evan said reaching over to hold her hand.

She squeezed his comforting grip and acknowledged Amelia. "I don't know what to say. I don't understand why everyone is being so nice to me."

Amelia smiled a genuine smile. "Because we care about you. You deserve to be cared about. You deserve respect and love. You are so good."

Mari got up from her seat at the same time Amelia did and they met for a warm embrace. "Thank you, Amelia. This means the world to me."

Taking their seats again, Marigold excitedly started making plans. "I can guarantee that I will make Miss Elinore's tea for her every day." Reflexively, upon sitting, she reached for Evan's hand again like it was part of her. He looked down at their joined hands and you could see the joy in his eyes.

Dallas spoke as he got up, "Evan, we need to head back in about five minutes. I'll wait for you in the kitchen."

Amelia looked at Mari to make sure she understood Mari's wish for a few minutes of semi-privacy with Evan. "I'll be in the kitchen, too."

Amelia met Dallas loading dishes into the dishwasher. They began working together as a team. It's what they did best. They could see the animated interaction of the young couple and it made all of their work to get to this point absolutely worth it. It was just too bad every case didn't end this well.

It had been a joyous day. Dallas and Amelia went to bed that night with a sense of completeness that could rarely be matched. The loose ends were tied up. It was case closed.

There had been other assignments mentioned in the past days. Several sounded interesting and just as urgent as this one had been. People needed their help. Bad things were happening every day. As they lay in bed, they discussed whether Amelia would join in another operation. It was dangerous, there was no question about that.

"It was quite exciting." Amelia stated. "I didn't like being away from you though."

"I was always there. In the shadows."

"You were, but it's too dark without you by my side."

They discussed several possible cases and the risks that came with each one. Was she willing to take the chance again? Something could go wrong at any time. Was she willing to get so far out of her comfort zone again? There had been several times that she wasn't sure she had made the right decisions. Was it worth the risk of things being completely out of her control in order to possibly help others the way they had helped those affected this time?

As she closed her eyes and started drifting off to sleep, she felt the corners of her mouth slowly turn up into a slight smile. She knew the answers to her questions. Of course, she knew the answers.

Made in the USA
Monee, IL
31 May 2025

18338623R00148